# PRAISE FOR M. L. BUCHMAN

3x Top 10 Romance of the Year

— ALA BOOKLIST

Tom Clancy fans open to a strong female lead will clamor for more.

— DRONE, PUBLISHERS WEEKLY

(Miranda Chase is) one of the most compelling, addicting, fascinating characters in any genre since the Monk television series.

— DRONE, ERNEST DEMPSEY

(*Drone* is) the best military thriller I've read in a very long time. Love the female characters.

— SHELDON MCARTHUR, FOUNDER
OF THE MYSTERY BOOKSTORE, LA

Superb!

— DRONE, BOOKLIST, STARRED
REVIEW

A fabulous soaring thriller.

— TAKE OVER AT MIDNIGHT,<br>MIDWEST BOOK REVIEW

Meticulously researched, hard-hitting, and suspenseful.

— PURE HEAT, PUBLISHERS WEEKLY,<br>STARRED REVIEW

The first…of (a) stellar, long-running (military) romantic suspense series.

— THE NIGHT IS MINE, BOOKLIST,<br>THE 20 BEST ROMANTIC SUSPENSE<br>NOVELS: MODERN MASTERPIECES

Expert technical details abound, as do realistic military missions with superb imagery that will have readers feeling as if they are right there in the midst and on the edges of their seats.

— LIGHT UP THE NIGHT, RT<br>REVIEWS, 4 1/2 STARS

Buchman has catapulted his way to the top tier of my favorite authors.

— FRESH FICTION

M L. Buchman's ability to keep the reader right in the middle of the action is amazing.

— LONG AND SHORT REVIEWS

The only thing you'll ask yourself is, "When does the next one come out?"

— WAIT UNTIL MIDNIGHT,<br>ROMANTIC TIMES BOOK REVIEWS, 4<br>STARS

I knew the books would be good, but I didn't realize how good.

— NIGHT STALKERS SERIES, KIRKUS<br>REVIEWS

# THE COMPLETE NIGHT STALKERS 5E STORIES

## A MILITARY ROMANCE SHORT STORY COLLECTION

### M. L. BUCHMAN

Buchman Bookworks

SIGN UP FOR M. L. BUCHMAN'S
NEWSLETTER TODAY

*and receive:*
*Release News*
*Free Short Stories*
*a Free Book*

*Get your free book today. Do it now.*
*free-book.mlbuchman.com*

# Other works by M. L. Buchman: *(* - also in audio)*

### Thrillers

**Dead Chef**
*One Chef!*
*Two Chef!*

**Miranda Chase**
*Drone**
*Thunderbolt**
*Condor**
*Ghostrider**

### Romantic Suspense

**Delta Force**
*Target Engaged**
*Heart Strike**
*Wild Justice**
*Midnight Trust**

**Firehawks**
MAIN FLIGHT
*Pure Heat*
*Full Blaze*
*Hot Point**
*Flash of Fire**
*Wild Fire*

SMOKEJUMPERS
*Wildfire at Dawn**
*Wildfire at Larch Creek**
*Wildfire on the Skagit**

**The Night Stalkers**
MAIN FLIGHT
*The Night Is Mine*
*I Own the Dawn*
*Wait Until Dark*
*Take Over at Midnight*
*Light Up the Night*
*Bring On the Dusk*
*By Break of Day*

AND THE NAVY
*Christmas at Steel Beach*
*Christmas at Peleliu Cove*
WHITE HOUSE HOLIDAY
*Daniel's Christmas**
*Frank's Independence Day**
*Peter's Christmas**
*Zachary's Christmas**
*Roy's Independence Day**
*Damien's Christmas**
5E
*Target of the Heart*
*Target Lock on Love*
*Target of Mine*
*Target of One's Own*

**Shadow Force: Psi**
*At the Slightest Sound**
*At the Quietest Word**

**White House Protection Force**
*Off the Leash**
*On Your Mark**
*In the Weeds**

### Contemporary Romance

**Eagle Cove**
*Return to Eagle Cove*
*Recipe for Eagle Cove*
*Longing for Eagle Cove*
*Keepsake for Eagle Cove*

**Henderson's Ranch**
*Nathan's Big Sky**
*Big Sky, Loyal Heart**
*Big Sky Dog Whisperer**

**Love Abroad**
*Heart of the Cotswolds: England*
*Path of Love: Cinque Terre, Italy*

# Other works by M. L. Buchman:

## Contemporary Romance (cont)

### Where Dreams
*Where Dreams are Born*
*Where Dreams Reside*
*Where Dreams Are of Christmas*
*Where Dreams Unfold*
*Where Dreams Are Written*

## Science Fiction / Fantasy

### Deities Anonymous
*Cookbook from Hell: Reheated*
*Saviors 101*

### Single Titles
*The Nara Reaction*
*Monk's Maze*
*the Me and Elsie Chronicles*

## Non-Fiction

### Strategies for Success
*Managing Your Inner Artist/Writer*
*Estate Planning for Authors*
*Character Voice*


# Short Story Series by M. L. Buchman:

## Romantic Suspense

### Delta Force
*Delta Force*

### Firehawks
*The Firehawks Lookouts*
*The Firehawks Hotshots*
*The Firebirds*

### The Night Stalkers
*The Night Stalkers*
*The Night Stalkers 5E*
*The Night Stalkers CSAR*
*The Night Stalkers Wedding Stories*

### US Coast Guard
*US Coast Guard*

### White House Protection Force
*White House Protection Force*

## Contemporary Romance

### Eagle Cove
*Eagle Cove*

### Henderson's Ranch
*Henderson's Ranch*

### Where Dreams
*Where Dreams*

## Thrillers

### Dead Chef
*Dead Chef*

## Science Fiction / Fantasy

### Deities Anonymous
*Deities Anonymous*

### Other
*The Future Night Stalkers*
*Single Titles*

# CONTENTS

# ABOUT THIS BOOK

*First there was the 160th Night Stalkers 5th Battalion D Company.*

*Then they formed the 5E. The few who knew about them called them "E for Extreme." After the four novels followed their adventures and romances came…*

*All five of the short stories of the 5E, their adventures and their love stories.*

- ***Love Behind the Lines***
- ***Flying Over the Waves***
- ***Since the First Day***
- ***Christmas Lights Objective***
- ***Sergeant George and the Dragoon***

*One great collection.*
*(Includes exclusive introductions to each story.)*

# INTRODUCTION

In the beginning, there was the Night Stalkers.

I had written several books in a variety of genres before the one that really captured my imagination and, as a bonus, launched my career.

*The Night Is Mine,* the first book in The Night Stalkers, was my first major success. It launched to rave reviews and I followed it happily with many titles following the adventures of US Army Majors Emily Beale and Mark Henderson. Their crew came to life across numerous novels and short stories.

While I wasn't really paying attention, the teams began spinning off into new series. Some close to home: The Night Stalkers White House, The Night Stalkers and the Navy. Some less close: Firehawks, Delta Force. They also inspired numerous short story series.

Amongst all of this proliferation, I learned a great deal about the Night Stalkers, both real and fictional.

In real life, the US Army 160th Special Operations Aviation Regiment (airborne)—SOAR(a)—are the most elite helicopter fliers anywhere. They are tasked with delivering America's very top teams anywhere they need to go. Delta Force and DEVGRU (SEAL Team 6) are their main customers. And by anywhere, they mean *anywhere*. The Night Stalkers also get their customers back out—from anywhere. Need to get into bin Laden's Pakistan compound? That was them. As well as: Panama, Takur Ghar, and a host of others. Need extraction from an out-of-control battle? They'll be there. And they'll touch down within thirty seconds of when they promised.

I am simply in awe of these fliers.

And as I learned more about the real-life exploits of these amazing men and women, the more I felt that I had shortchanged them in some ways.

Mark Henderson's 5th Battalion D Company fought noble fights, rescued orphans, and fell in love. Well, the last was a given, these are romance stories after all. Even the main series of short stories had a similar…feel to them.

I loved telling their stories. It was an immense amount of fun as well as the honor of paying even a glimmer of an homage to the real-life heroes.

However, there was another slice of stories that I found myself wanting to tell. Stories where the moral lines weren't so clear. Where the missions were more extreme, more challenging. Not just to the warrior, but also to the person inside the warrior.

From these desires were born the Night Stalkers 5E, 5th Battalion E Company—the "Extreme."

I provided the 5E with the very latest stealth helicopters.

I formed them not from the best of the best, the most shining warriors. Instead, I sought fighters who were tough—"diamonds in the rough" rather than already polished and shining. It let me dig into the evolution of a person far more deeply. Instead of merely becoming their best selves, I got to watch/help them grow into it. And make it clear that there was still more road out ahead of them, too.

Perhaps the 5D had been overly polished. Part of it was the natural idealization of a good romantic tale. But I think another part of it was that I was growing as a writer.

I also went looking for more dangerous missions. In the tales of the 5D (Mark Henderson's and Emily Beale's stories), my crews were occasionally assigned what I termed the "Black-in-black" missions.

A "White" mission or "White Op" is one that is reported to the news services.

A "Black Op" is one that is never supposed to come out, except perhaps after the fact, such as the takedown of Osama bin Laden. The Black Op is dominant in the world of the real-life 160th SOAR as well.

However, there are deeper and darker missions. For these I made up the name for the missions that could never be admitted to: Black-in-black. Not to the press, not to a commanding officer on the "outside" of the mission, not to anyone—ever.

They were a part of each Henderson and Beale novel, but they weren't the core.

As I kept telling the 5D stories, I liked the idea that the missions were top secret—but the 5E had a *further* goal: each mission should seem as if SOAR and US forces had never been there at all.

What if the 5E were *invisible?*

That gave birth to the novels and their wild settings:

- *Target of the Heart* – the heart of China
- *Target Lock on Love* – Russia Kamchatka Peninsula
- *Target of Mine* – a cruise ship and Honduras
- *Target of One's Own* – Senegal, Africa, and the Dakar Rally in South America

The short stories?

These are also in the vein of the "rougher diamond" and I hope they make you smile.

# LOVE BEHIND THE LINES

**_Lieutenant "Manny" Malcolm's_** _mission: Extract an embedded CIA agent from deep inside Russian Crimea. When a missile blows up his helicopter, it's a whole new mission._

**_Alisa, Irina, Lyudmila..._** _After wearing so many identities, does her true self even still exist? Betrayed by a trusted contact, her new assignment—survival!_

_Only together can they find Love Behind the Lines._

# INTRODUCTION

In the spirit of the 5E mentioned above, being invisible made me think of spies. Spies are specialists at being invisible…until something goes wrong. As a bonus, I'd never written about a spy before.

Though the story was written in 2016, its origins stem from two real-life events in 2014.

In 2014, a White House press officer accidentally released the name of the US's top spy in Afghanistan in an email that went to 6,000 journalists. The US press assisted in suppressing the release, but it was a major miscarriage of protocol for the intelligence services—endangering the agent, as well as his wife and family.

Also in 2014, the Russians annexed the Crimea. Some of this was due to a percentage of the population being Russian, but most of it was due to a massive infiltration of Russian troops. They wore no troop insignia, wearing unmarked, nondescript military uniforms. They became known as "the little green men" for that reason. They were easily identified by their weapons, tactics, and lethality as Spetsnaz—the Russian

Special Operations equivalent of Delta Force and 75th Rangers.

Most of the Ukrainian military was fully replaced, but a few who'd helped topple their own government were retained.

And there I found my story.

The female spy, the man sent in to extract her, and the corrupt ex-Ukrainian military of the Crimea after Russian annexation.

---

"*Mission recall. Repeat, mission* recall."

"You've got to be shitting me." Lieutenant Manfred "M&M" Malcolm looked down at the radio to make sure that it was on tonight's frequency and that the message wasn't for someone else.

"I'm only three goddamn klicks out!" He shouted at the radio, though he didn't hit his transmit key to send his least fond regards. There were some places that American military helicopters should never be caught and he was in one of them. His Little Bird MH-6 was stealth rigged and his radio signal was encrypted…but that wouldn't make him or the point of origin of any electronic transmission invisible.

"Mission X-ray Tango Alpha is aborted," the Air Mission Commander repeated. "Return to base."

XTA. Extraction of prime target Alpha. That was his mission tonight.

"Goddamn it!" He hated the alphabet agencies. DIA, NSA, and most particularly the CIA. They never seemed to know what they wanted. In the military, you received a mission, you planned it, and you by god executed it after you were given the "Go!" order. In the CIA he figured they had a mission board and flung darts at it until they hit something and said, "Oh, let's do that." He'd bet they wore blindfolds while planning or whatever it was they did back in Langley. After that, because shit flowed downhill, it would be:

"Hey Manny," as if pretending they were already on a first-name basis before they'd even talked and he didn't have a rank after a decade of flying and even facing down Officer Candidate School. "We have a top level asset"—which meant spy—"whose cover is blown. We need an immediate extraction. Tonight."

There were only two companies in the entire US military able to fly a route like the one needed, SOAR's 5D and his own 5E. The helicopters of the Special Operations Aviation Regiment's 5th Battalion E Company had been in a better position so he'd been sent in.

Now he was deep behind Russian lines—except the Russians still insisted they weren't in Crimea—and he had to figure out how to get back without tripping some high-tech booby trap. All that noise about the Russians being so far behind in tech was just that, noise. Their problem was that they couldn't afford as much of the good shit as America could, but what they had was damned impressive. And those heavy-duty assets were concentrated in places of particular importance to the Russian government…like every square meter within a hundred klicks of his present position just outside of Sevastopol, Crimea. Which had been part of the Ukraine until recently. He wished it still was, because then he'd be welcome instead of being a target.

Low and fast had been his answer going in; he just hoped that it would work equally well on his passage out. He yanked up on the collective and shoved the cyclic forward to lay the hammer down hard.

That hope lasted almost thirteen seconds.

Some Russian soldier with an itchy trigger finger and thirty-year old technology fired a missile at his trace. It was a crazy waste of $100,000 *Igla* surface-to-air missile, because Manny knew that his craft's radar signature wasn't much bigger than a fat seagull's. It was a stupid move by an undertrained *molodoy;* an action for which he'd probably be punished above and beyond standard new-recruit hazing. Any soldier with a decent amount of training would have ignored that faint blip on the tracking radar.

What the goddamn, suffering *molodoy* would never know was that he'd actually done his job exactly right.

Once on Manny's tail, there was only so much that could be done to disguise the thousand degrees of heat exhaust from his turbine engine. The missile had flown close enough to sniff out that heat signature and zeroed in. It moved at almost Mach 2 and he moved at about one-tenth of that.

A locked-on *Igla* wasn't something that was evaded by a quick maneuver. The "needle" as it was aptly named, was about to drill his ass. It ignored the signal-blocking chaff that Manny dispersed. Firing off a round of distracting flares would illuminate and pinpoint his location for much more substantial forces. He saw only one chance and punched for it. Head for the sea.

The high cliffs south of Sevastopol were just close

enough for him to dive over the edge and buy himself a few seconds before the missile reacquired. A half kilometer out from shore, he stalled the helicopter hard, heaving back on the cyclic until the joystick was jammed into his gut. His Little Bird groaned and wept, but it slammed from a hundred and seventy-five miles an hour to under forty in moments.

He armed the self-destruct charges, unsnapped his belt, and dove out the doorway.

He was less than halfway to the water when the *Igla* caught up with his Little Bird. The explosion was blinding in its reflection off the water, the concussive punch of combined missile and destruct charges made the last twenty-five feet of his fall go by very quickly.

2

*I**t felt as if* Alisa had been undercover her entire life. First from the ruling government of the Prime Minister turned dictator and now from the Russians. Their recent annexation of Crimea had made her job a hundred times more dangerous and she stayed because she didn't know what else to do. She was trapped between the Russian SVR, their version of the CIA, who would ruin her day if her role was ever discovered, and the CIA itself with their promises of safe passage out…if she could just hold on a while longer and find out about whatever was next on their never-ending list.

Then Sergey of the SVR had taken a sudden interest in her, more than just trying to bed her. He began dropping by her desk at work, or just happening to run into her when she was out at a club.

Knowing she'd reached her limit, she'd finally convinced the CIA that it was time to honor their commitment and send in an extraction team as she had no way of escaping on her own.

For twenty hours she'd cowered in fear, dodging shadows and afraid at each moment that she'd be taken into custody and never see daylight again. Just as she was preparing to leave and work her slow way to the extraction rendezvous—a journey that would take half the night—a knock had sounded on her door.

Instead a phalanx of guards, there had been only Sergey. He had offered to "protect" her in exchange for certain "services." She didn't need to watch where his eyes remained fixed to know what services he was interested in and didn't care to guess how brief a respite from prison his protection would offer should she consent.

Then Sergey had made the mistake—fatal as it turned out—of tapping his briefcase and saying he had a report he would turn in if she did not agree.

She had read the report while Sergey quietly sank to the bottom of Pivdenna Bay. He had gotten only a few facts right, but two of them were completely damning— they also told her who among her informants must be a double agent for the SVR, as that part of the report was too accurate. When she found the thumb drive in his pants pocket, with a copy of the report on it, she decided that Sergey was definitely arrogant enough to have left no form of "Open this file if I do not return" at the office.

Just in case, Alisa would have to die tonight along with the ever-so-surprised Sergey. Irina (still a top-twenty name among Ukrainian women) would be born tomorrow with fresh papers and a new address. She had deep connections in both the "renegade terrorist" Ukrainian camp and the Russian "our special forces

Spetsnaz aren't really here" camp (to which Sergey had belonged).

If Sergey had truly kept everything to himself, then there was only one person who still could expose her, Lesia Melnyk. Lesia was General Vlad Kozlov's mistress and worked in the same department as Alisa. She had been Alisa's first friend in a long time and the betrayal cut deep.

Alisa decided that except for Lesia she was safe enough. Her thinking was that with Sergey's demise and his report gone, an identity change should be enough to protect her. She could stay and continue running her other contacts, so she called off the extraction.

The other reason to stay was as unprofessional as hell and she didn't care. Lesia was her supposed best friend and the first person she'd turned, or thought she had. Alisa wanted revenge—badly.

Alisa put the thumb drive in her pocket. A glance around the apartment hurt so much. She wanted to take everything and could take nothing. She slipped her parents' photo in her pocket, tossed the paper copy of Sergey's report along with a couple recent copies of *Pravda* on top of her stove, set the burners on high, and left quickly.

By the time she had walked a block away, her one-bedroom *kvartira* (rather than *kvartyra* as Sevastopol was no longer a Ukrainian city but rather a Russian one) was on fire. When she glanced back two blocks later, it was engulfed and flames were streaming out the windows. She wore a dead man's clothes, which weren't a bad fit except for being very tight across the chest even without a bra (it would have helped if Sergey had worked out more in life), and had her long blond hair tucked up into a worker's cap. The May weather was too warm for a *ushanka* fur hat. She'd liked that hat and hated to leave it behind in the flames.

For three nameless hours, she slouched her way across the city and back. No longer Alisa and not yet Irina, she watched carefully for a tail.

After that she sat for an hour in the back of Zeppelin Club. It was Friday night and the work-week crowd was blowing out as desperately as they could. The loud Euro pop was predictably awful though the "exotic" female dancers managed to not look too bored. Her stool at a small table along the far side of the stage allowed her to watch the entrance between the dancers' bare legs and other body parts as they arched and writhed. It was hard to believe, but perhaps Sergey really had been dumb enough to confront a foreign agent without a backup.

She spent another hour drinking at a shadowed table in a porn club, the favorite of one of her contacts, but gave up around four a.m. while the party was still rolling hard (pun intended). She staggered her way back past Alisa's apartment. The fire brigade had been and gone. The burned shell would reveal nothing that would arouse suspicions except for its no-longer-existent renter's failure to return. No one waited in the shadows looking for a woman with long blond hair and serious curves. And certainly not for a drunken man staggering homeward.

She hadn't meant to drink as much as she did, though it was the leading national pastime. That, and griping about the brutal Russians or the lazy Ukrainians —depending on who you were drinking with: the noble Ukrainians or the world-conquering Russians. But the nerves had gotten to her. She'd made it through the Russian invasion of Crimea more calmly than facing exposure by Sergey. Had he been just one tiny bit less interested in her breasts, she'd probably be screaming in an SVR torture cell at the moment.

And if she'd been one bit less angry at Lesia Melnyk, she'd have climbed on the damned helicopter and been safe by now. But the anger had grown rather than abating. The alcohol buffered none of the emotions ripping at her.

She leaned her head against the door of the safe house, just three streets over from her burned-out apartment, and struggled to catch her breath. Her hands were shaky as she reached for her keys.

Purse, where was her purse?

No, dressed as a man now.

Pants pocket.

Key in door, the soft click of the lock.

And at the same moment a soft sound behind her, then a jabbing pressure in the middle of her back.

"*Medlenno,*" a voice commanded in Russian. Slowly indeed.

*anny eased **through the** doorway and kept his Glock 19 pressed against the man's back until they were both inside. He'd been through far too much shit in the last ten hours to trust anyone, safe house or not.

Impossibly, he hadn't died despite his helicopter being shot down by a missile. However, the explosion had happened less than a thousand meters from a Russian frigate, so there was no way for Quinn and Patty in the backup helo to fish his ass out of the water without being targeted themselves.

The Russians had been slow to arrive and inspect the explosion area, which had allowed him time to swim to shore unobserved. Then the CIA had tried stonewalling on the location of their safe house. That had given him his first smile as he hid at the base of a Crimean cliff, carefully covered in sand except for his face despite the nighttime darkness. He wouldn't want to be one of Langley's CIA headquarters personnel right now, not with his 5E commanders Pete Napier and

Daniella Delacroix after them. They'd coughed up the safe house address eventually.

Manny had made selections from a couple of clotheslines and then simply walked across the city. Sometimes brash paid off. No one stopped him, except for his nerves which had attempted to asphyxiate him at every step. When he'd arrived, the door was locked. He really hated Crimea.

The CIA's passive-aggressive goddamn joke, not telling him where to find the key. If he ever met the bastard who—

Unproductive thinking!

The ground floor was totally locked and barred.

He'd climbed up to a small balcony, that was equally fortified, and squatted down while he tried to figure out what to do. The traffic was light in this neighborhood at oh-four-bumfuck in the morning, just some drunk weaving his lazy ass home.

Then the drunk had stepped up to the safe house door directly below Manny's balcony. He waited until the man almost had the door open, then dropped down and crowded him inside.

Once through the door, he shoved the drunk up against the wall. If this was the caliber of men the CIA could find, it was no wonder the Russians had moved in so easily.

The house was quiet and dark. The very first light of dawn filtered weakly through a small window set above the door, just enough to see shapes.

Without moving his weapon, Manny kicked the man's feet apart and forced him to raise his hands, palm-flat, against the wall. Then he began checking out the man. A vicious flick-blade in his sock. Manny almost missed the thin strap for the hideaway holster inside his thigh—for hidden carry but not quick draw, he'd pants the guy in a moment and take it. Then he reached to check the crotch, but there was nothing there.

The drunk began cursing in slurred Russian, but he nudged his sidearm hard against his kidney…no, her kidney…and the Russian grunted and began complaining louder.

"*Zatknis!*"

The drunk woman continued to grumble, but she did so more quietly. He reached around to undo her belt and pants enough to recover the hidden weapon. Her jacket gave up nothing except a thumb drive which he pocketed. Then he yanked the jacket off her and tossed it aside just in case he'd missed something. Another blade, this time tucked down between ample breasts, and a shower of long hair when he knocked the cap aside. He couldn't feel anything inside the cap except a photo that it was too dark to see.

He eased away until he was well out of reach with his back against the front door so that there would be no surprises. Then he flicked on a light on a small table.

"Turn. Slowly," he said in Russian.

"Your accent. It is terrible," the woman mumbled in heavily-inflected English as she turned.

"So sue me."

She rolled over, still leaning against the wall for support, until her back was pressed against it. Without the jacket, her men's clothing didn't mask a thing about her. Trim, built, long blond hair that cascaded past her shoulders, and piercing blue eyes in a lovely face.

"Damn. I can see I should have visited Crimea sooner."

"Go and take yourself to hells, Yankee. Who are you?"

"Prince Charming. And it's 'to hell' but you're too late, I'm already there. Who are you?"

"I do not know this anymore," her voice wavered. "Call me the Grand Duchess Anastasia for all I care," then the woman slid down the wall to sit on her butt. "Nothing left but ashes." She rubbed at her face then leaned her head back against the plaster. Her hands dropped into her lap.

Manny felt as exhausted as she looked. He'd been running mostly on adrenalin since they'd woken him at this time yesterday morning, a thousand kilometers away.

Her head tipped slightly to one side.

Then she softly began to snore.

Manny really, really hated Crimea.

## 4

*A*lisa woke slowly.

Except she wasn't Alisa anymore. She was… Irina now. Irina. Had to repeat her new name until it was second nature. Irina Kovalenko. Irina Kovalenko.

Irina remembered her apartment burning, no, her torching her own apartment. She remembered…

*Chyort voz'mi!* She remembered slitting Sergey's throat. She'd managed to lead him down to an out of the way dock along the waterfront after convincing him that taking her out to dinner was a sure path to success with her—thankfully Sevastopol was mostly waterfront.

While he'd been enjoying himself, groping her breasts with brutal strength, she'd slipped a blade up through the soft underpart of his chin and managed to cut his brainstem just like in training. For a moment he'd squeezed her breasts so convulsively hard that she was the one who almost cried out. Then he let go and slumped to the planking.

She'd stripped him, tied an anchor that she stole

from one of the boats about his ankles, and quietly disposed of the first person she'd ever killed.

But she'd held it together, by God. She'd made it back to her apartment, studied his report, made a plan, and executed her escape.

She made good until…the man at the door. He'd come out of nowhere. She'd had no tail; she was certain of it.

And then there'd been a gun at her back.

An American man who—

Irina tried to sit up—and flopped back on the mattress. Now that she'd tried to move, she could feel the ropes about her wrist and ankles. Not tight but, she pulled on them, not giving either.

"*Der'mo!*" She opened her eyes. *Oh shit!*

She was in a small, dingy bedroom. A battered dresser. A small, dust-hazed mirror. The ugliest wallpaper on the planet, blue with large red roses, that was peeling at the corners.

And a bed, the one she was tied to. Her wrists were above her head, not uncomfortably so, but too far to reach the knots with her teeth. Her ankles were tied, but she could still feel her toes, so the circulation wasn't cut off. A slight motion and she could tell that she still wore a shirt and her panties, but none of her weapons. A blanket lay over her, a woolen one. It itched.

If this was an SVR prison cell, it was much more luxurious than she'd expected. If this was a hotel…it sucked!

She raised her head to look about more carefully. Beyond the foot of the bed a man slumped deep in a battered armchair. He was slender, with dark hair that needed a trim. He needed a shave as well. His sidearm was on his lap, his booted feet were crossed on the foot of her bed, and his dark eyes were watching her.

"Bet you feel like shit," his voice was low and painfully astute.

Her hangover sprang to the foreground. "*Spasibo, parshiviy.* I had not noticed."

"You're welcome and I'm only an asshole when I'm in the mood. At the moment, I'm totally there. You know, it's not your average person who falls asleep at gunpoint."

"Long day," she countered.

"Tell me about it."

She closed her eyes and swore to herself that she'd never drink vodka again.

"Seriously, tell me about it. Start with your name."

"My name is Irina," Irina what? Started with a K. "Irina Kovalenko." Her gaff shouldn't be too noticeable. "Had too much to drink."

"That explains the night, now tell me about the day."

She opened her eyes long enough to glare at him. A light curtain across the window kept her from telling what time of day it was, though it was still bright enough to hurt. She closed her eyes and let her head drop back to the pillow again.

"Who are *you, tolstak?*" Because she wasn't about to tell some unknown fat-ass about her day.

5

"*Interesting place you have* here, Grand Duchess." Manny made it conversational when it became clear she wasn't going to say anything more.

She looked at him strangely when he called her that. Too far gone last night to remember naming herself as the youngest of the old Czar's children.

Once he'd been sure that she wasn't feigning sleep, he'd stripped her outer clothes, tied her to the bed, and tucked her in. Then he'd investigated the house.

The interior dimensions hadn't matched the exterior and it hadn't taken him long to figure out why. First and second floor each had hidden rooms, subtle ones, not easy to notice. Except he'd been trained by the very best instructors the US Army had on room clearing techniques—including identifying and opening hidden spaces. One space was packed with clothing in multiple sexes and sizes. He selected a few pieces that fit better than what he'd been able to scavenge off the clothesline.

The other space had weapons, a nice forgery setup for making false passports, and a few radios.

He'd also found a laptop and checked out the thumb drive he'd taken from her pocket. If she'd done even half of what was in the report he found there, he was impressed as hell. But it didn't mean that he trusted her either.

"Not my place," the blond mumbled without opening her eyes. Christ, he could look at her all day. Even hungover she was a knockout. While crossing the city last night he'd noted that Ukrainian women were on the whole exceptionally attractive, but she was above and beyond.

"CIA's I assume, since they sent me here. Yet you had a key. What's a drunken trollop doing with a key to a CIA safe house?"

"I am no a drunken trollop!" She was angry enough to ignore her hangover and glare at him, at least one eye's worth. He took pity on her and reached over to close one of the heavier curtains. "What is trollop?" She asked in a much gentler tone.

"Whatever you say, Duchess. You were skunk-drunk last night, and parading around in men's clothes without a bra despite your impressive figure. Now who the hell *are* you?" He'd had enough of stupid games. "And try to come up with a real name this time."

She sighed. "If I do, will you get me some aspirin?"

"Sure. Might even let you take it too, Duchess."

"You would make lousy interrogator for SVR. No call me that."

"Whatever you say, Duchess. But I'm one hell of a pilot."

That brought her head back up to look at him, "Pilot for the Americans? The Night Stalkers?"

He started to nod and then could only think of one way she could know that. It jolted him to his feet clenching his weapon.

She cringed, so he slammed the pistol into his belt. He'd left his holster in the back of a handy police cruiser last night—which was bound to confuse the crap out of them though it had no markings on it.

"You bitch!" She flinched as if he'd struck her. He'd never hit a woman, but he was awfully tempted to strangle one at the moment. "You cancelled an extract less than sixty seconds from pickup?"

"No! I call three hours before. Three hours!"

Manny didn't even know how to answer that.

It eventually led him to his untying her and the two of them sitting across the kitchen table from each other. It had one leg too short and kept rocking back and forth as they both drank burned coffee made with ancient grounds. The kitchen was as disreputable as the table and the only food was a bag of rice that probably had been there since before the Soviet Union had imploded.

They determined that their watches were in sync. The abort-mission command had taken three hours (minus sixty seconds) to worm its way out of Langley and out to the field. Insane. Manny knew the Night Stalkers wouldn't have delayed such a message; they'd know the risk.

"Goddamn spooks," he couldn't help complaining.

"Spooks? Ah, spies. I too am spy, but I am agreeing very much."

He smiled. It was hard not to smile at her. And not just because of her physical attributes. He enjoyed her in-your-face personality—milquetoast, quiet women never did it for him and she was anything but. Plus, he certainly did like the way she looked in just a men's shirt, underwear, and socks. If she thought she was playing him by not getting fully dressed, it wasn't going to work —but he wasn't going to file any complaints about the scenery. For some reason the plain white socks just made the whole outfit real damn cute.

She rested her elbows on the grimy table and leaned her head down into her hands. Her shirt hung forward and the scenery got a whole lot better. The upper part of her breasts were full, creamy…and bore dark patches the size of fingerprints.

"Who marked you, Grand Duchess?"

"I tell you to stop—" She glanced up at him, noticed the direction of his attention, then scowled before looking down at her own chest. "*Moodak!* That bloody dead bastard!"

And she told him about the unlamented Sergey and the burned-out apartment.

"If your cover was gone, why the hell did you cancel the extract?"

"You supposed to save me, but you shot from sky?" She teased him. "Not the kind of hero-pilot a good girl is looking for."

"Then what kind of hero-pilot is 'a good girl' looking for?"

6

---

*This girl was enjoying* the hero-pilot sitting just across from her. He kept surprising her. Soon she might be telling him her real story. Actually, probably no reason not to. Why not.

"I am Lyudmila Bykov. That is truth. I'm am named for Lyudmila the most famous woman sniper ever. She kill many German and Romanians here, in Sevastopol, during the World War Second. I am also pissed-off war orphan. Pissed-off, yes?"

Manny nodded that she'd gotten it right.

"I am nineteen when the Prime Minister Yanukovych enforcers put down the supporters of opposition leader Yulia Tymoshenko. Yulia want closer ties to NATO and was jailed for it. Everybody except Russia declare her trial all bad. Unfair. My parents were very close to Yulia and were executed in their beds by 'criminals unknown.' A CIA recruiter found me when I was very drunk and very, very pissed-off. With their help I change my name, I start working here as coordinator, to help in government offices, with Russian Black Sea

Fleet. You know they are stationed here? In Sevastopol?"

"I almost got to see them up close and personal last night," and she didn't like the darkness of the frown on his face. Ever since he had untied her, he had looked relaxed and cheerful. But she did not forget the gun that was still sticking out from his belt and she could see the anger still there. She was glad it was not aimed at her.

"I still work in office. No, no more. Last night I killed Alisa and became Irinia."

"Who is really Lyudmila. Good story, Grand Duchess."

"Why do you keep calling me this?"

Manny shrugged as he crossed to the stove. His movements were quick and precise. It was the third time he had freshened their coffees though neither of them were drinking much. She had the feeling that he wasn't very good at sitting still. Usually she wasn't either, but the aspirin hadn't gone to her head.

"Where did you learn such good English?"

"Parents. They buy me tutor so I'm ready to ready to serve in Tymoshenko's government. As I say, true believers for all the no good it did them."

"So how to get out of here?" Manny was pacing about the kitchen.

"Out of where?"

"Crimea."

She looked up at him, "I'm not leaving."

"You don't *look* stupid."

"There's someone who betrayed me. I have to deal with that." She was going to take Lesia Melnyk apart if it was the last thing she did to that *sooka!*

"You going to end up dead in the process?"

She didn't have a good answer to that.

This time Manny came to a stop. He squatted close in front of her. "There's got to be a better choice than staying for revenge, Lyudmila."

If there was, she couldn't think of it. Hope was something she had stopped believing in long before Sergey and his report.

"My parents called me Mila," and she did her best not to cry. Perhaps she would see them soon…too bad she didn't believe in that either.

7

*It rapidly became clear* to Manny that he wasn't going to make it out of Sevastopol alive without Mila's help. She made a few discreet inquiries among her friends and Russian security was way up since the destruction of his helicopter. Nobody knew *what* had exploded outside their harbor, but their increased readiness eliminated any rescue by air. And by sea was even dodgier, which was why they'd risked the extraction by air in the first place.

"Sometimes the only way out is through," he had to solve this.

For two days they barely slept as they strategized, discarding theories and escape routes as fast as they thought them up.

"There's no way that cutting your hair and dying it black would buy you more than a few days. It didn't work in the Jason Bourne movies. It won't work for you, Duchess. You're too goddamn beautiful. And if you don't show up for work on Monday, all sorts of alarms will going off."

After the initial sadness that had almost broken his heart to watch, Mila rallied. Her knowledge of government and the Russian military was deep…and not helping.

"Maybe our ticket out of here is the woman who betrayed you. Tell me about your traitor"—weird thing to say to a spy. "This Lesia who informed on you to the SVR. We have to figure this out."

When he said "we" she'd shot him a smile that could have lit up the sky.

"What?"

"For almost a decade it has been 'me'," her voice was an intimate whisper. "You said 'we'."

"That's how the world spins," he spoke quickly to cover what he really wanted to do next.

He crossed to the window to get a little more distance.

"I've got a team out there working the problem for me," he waved toward the back of the building next door, an abandoned warehouse.

His team had fed him several ideas during very brief radio calls, though none had panned out yet.

"The whole world doesn't work like the Russians and the CIA. Hell, I thought Patty and Quinn were going to fly right into the Russians' guns to extract me. I had to risk the radio to call them off while I was swimming for shore."

And when he was sure that he once again had control of himself, they went back to their planning, but it had changed. It had changed from 'me' to 'we' in a way that Manny hadn't anticipated. High pressure situation be damned, every single thing he learned about Grand Duchess Lyudmila of Sevastopol, the more he appreciated her. At a level of risk that only a Night Stalker could understand, she had fed a constant stream of actionable intelligence to the West. It hadn't been enough to save Crimea from the Russians, but it had probably saved the rest of the country from invasion.

By Sunday night they had a plan.

It was shaky as hell, but they had one.

When they were both too weary to think up another contingency, they'd dropped down side by side on a couch in what could laughably be called a living room.

"What do you think our chances are? To survival?"

Manny shrugged, "Anyone else, thirty percent at best. You and me, Duchess? I'm betting my life on it being a hundred."

"Are you always so positive?"

"Never saw much fun in focusing on the other side of that coin. I mess up plenty, but that's not where I live."

"That is good," she nodded to herself, then nodded again. Her hair a slick slide of gold that he wanted to toy with every time she moved. "It's not what I have done in past, but it's what I will do in future. What about after?"

"You mean after, as in if we get out of this alive?"

8

*S*he poked him in the ribs, "*When* we get out of this alive." She liked the intimacy of the gesture.

"Right. Well, I've got some buddies who would love to meet you."

Mila could feel her skin go cold. She knew what kind of "buddies" people wanted to introduce pretty blonds to. It had served her well as a spy in the Ukraine, but Alisa, Irina, and Lyudmila were all three sick of being used for their body.

"They're in this odd little intelligence group with no name. Finding a trained insider in Ukrainian politics, fluent in English and Russian…they're definitely going to want to meet you."

"That…" wasn't what she'd been expecting. "Do they work with you very much?" Or would he be far away if she worked with them?

Manny was nodding. "That's kind of their purpose. It would be nice if…"

She could hear him taper off, as if worried that he'd

crossed some line. He was the strangest man she'd ever met.

First, she hadn't woken up naked and being raped.

Once he'd released her—which he had done long before she would have if their roles had been reversed—she'd waited through the first day, expecting it to happen anyway. Or at least sex to happen; he didn't strike her as a cruel man.

But by now, they'd rarely been more than a step apart for two days and still he'd done nothing, though the way he watched her there was no question he'd wanted to.

Well, now she wanted to as well. No matter what he said, their chances weren't good—their plan was simply the best of many terrible options.

She rose and, taking him by the hand, pulled him to his feet. Once they reached the bedroom, he did an incredible job of making her feel absolutely grand.

## 9

"**Hi, honey. Look who** *else* decided to come along with Lesia?"

Manny just about swallowed his tongue. Their plan had included a dinner with the woman who had betrayed Mila's—no, she was back to being Alisa for one more night—Alisa's trust.

Just her.

Instead, the two women were followed closely by a man in full military uniform who wore the one star and no red stripes insignia of a major general of the Russian Federation.

"This is Lesia. Who I told you so much about," Alisa was being a bubbly blond that he barely recognized, the party-girl facade worn by the Grand Duchess of sheer balls—bringing a major general to dinner. She turned to her former friend, a very attractive brunette. "And this is Manny. Isn't he just the cutest?"

That was a new one, but Manny wasn't going to argue.

Their escape plan was to convince Lesia to invite

them out to her dacha in the country…where she apparently played mistress with her lover the general. Once clear of Sevastopol and the heavy protection surrounding the Black Sea Fleet, they could signal Patty and Quinn to meet them at the dacha, backed up by the hammer blow of the 5E Company in close support.

However, Lesia had not come alone.

"And this is Vlad," the crazy blond hung onto the general's arm for a moment. "He's in charge of the Naval helicopter fleet at Kacha." Alisa said that last bit like it was a slightly confusing throwaway line, but Manny heard "helicopter fleet" loud and clear. In that moment he forgave Alisa everything. There had to be a way to use this.

He was suddenly damn glad that he'd arranged for the fliers of the 5E to hold at thirty kilometers out, pending his final call. He wanted to avoid a reenactment of three nights ago and it was a distance they could cover in six minutes or less. Who could predict where the evening was headed.

Dinner was a strange and surreal affair. Manny's role was pretending to be a foreign correspondent, a Canadian who had somehow finagled a visa into an area where no press were allowed. Except he knew nothing about being a reporter and his one trip to Canada had been a drunk weekend during the Stanley Cup hockey playoffs between the New York Rangers and the Montréal Canadiens.

The bait they'd dangled to get Lesia to the meal had been vague hints that Manny was only posing as a Canadian reporter and was actually Alisa's "big" contact. A next-tier intelligence coup that Lesia would be unable to resist. So unable to resist, that she'd brought the general along to share in the glory. Perhaps if she delivered both US agents, the unmentioned wife would become powerless and the beautiful Lesia would gain the Mrs. General prize.

Throughout the meal, Alisa teased and flirted outrageously. Rather than playing footsie under the table, as would fit the events going on above the table, she kept a constant hard pressure of her leg wrapped about his. He could tell her nerves were stretched right near the breaking point, almost as badly as the woman he'd met three days ago—drunk and dressed as a man.

But rather than showing it, she was magnificent. Sparkling, downright effervescent, and damned fun despite the crazy situation.

Not surprisingly, the dinner topic that he and Vlad landed on was helicopters. As long as that was the topic, Manny could pretend to be a war correspondent who knew about helicopters from various embeds he'd done with forward teams.

It took a while for Manny to realize that Vlad was out of the loop here. He was just under the impression that he was having a lively dinner with one of his mistress' friends. And he definitely liked Alisa. So much so that Manny was forced to pay more and more attention to the mistress so that she didn't become angry.

Then Alisa let slip that Manny had flown helicopters himself.

Military ones.

*What the hell?* He didn't catch on to what she could possibly be thinking until she nodded ever so slightly toward the general, at the same moment she kicked him sharply under the table.

After that the conversation shifted. He and General Vlad Kozlov were suddenly best buddies and soon Manny was dancing around the edges of what technologic insights he could share without violating his own Top Secret clearance.

And Lesia was, in his amateur-reporter opinion, no master spy. However, she was a very drunk one and was soon swept up in the chatter of their lively evening.

*lisa hung on for* the wild and drunken ride to Kacha Airbase. It turned out that nothing would do, after a little coaxing and a few teasing suggestions on her own part, except for General Vlad Kozlov to show Manny the latest technology out of Russia. It had just arrived and he was very proud of having it under his local command.

"I am only Ukrainian general that Russians keep," he'd boasted. "They trust me very much. I am most important Ukrainian man in Crimea military."

Thankfully being a major general also earned him a driver, a silent and sober man able to escort them safely across the twenty-kilometer transit from the restaurant to the base. The general was certainly in no condition to drive. He and Manny were singing together in some terrible mixture of three languages.

"It is beautiful machine. It will make Americans sick it so good," the general slipped back and forth between Ukrainian and Russian making his speech broken and slurred. Lesia was even worse off.

Alisa—she had to stay solidly in her Alisa mode just a while longer—wished she could drag Manny aside. First, she'd kiss him for being so magnificent at dinner. Truth be told, she couldn't wait to jump him. She'd been scared to death, but Manny had been so calm and smooth that everything had worked…so far.

That was the second thing she wanted to do: drag Manny aside and ask, "What the hell are we doing?" Any remnants of their original plan had been cleared off the table along with the *tabak börek* dumplings with broth and long before the arrival of the *pennik* apricot pie and the third bottle of Massandra wine—served with lots of vodka on the side.

Of course Manny was too sotted to answer. More than once he'd groped Lesia's breast instead of her own. It was ironic, considering how they'd met, that she was the only one still sober enough to care about such things.

But before she could collect her thoughts more than to recognize that the hand on her knee and working its way up her skirt was not Manny's, they arrived at the airbase.

Reacting to steadfast refusal on Manny's part, the general soon forced him into the pilot's seat then sat beside him in the copilot's seat. She and Lesia were placed close behind them at the engineering stations.

"This," Vlad slapped the top of the central console. "This is a Kamov Ka-35 Airborne Early Warning platform. With this, we can see ballistic missile, submarine launch, ship launch, American helicopter…" He nudged Manny with an elbow and apparently thought he was lowering his voice, though he wasn't.

"We can even see what our women would hide from us but is there for a man's taking. *Da? Da?*"

"Yes!" Manny agreed with a fist pump.

The general tried to copy the gesture but was so drunk that he cracked his elbow hard on the door. Lesia had passed out in her seat.

"Should we take it up for a test?" Manny asked in an oddly meek tone, then he turned and winked at her—very soberly.

*Take it up for a…* Oh my god! Manny was brilliant. The newest Russian technology could take them out of Crimea…and it would be a major coup to deliver it to the American technicians for study. There wouldn't even be any political fallout as it would look like the general and his mistress were defecting. If this worked, the Americans would also get everything Lesia and Vlad knew.

Manny winked again and nodded toward the general.

*Oh!*

"Please, Vlad," Alisa poured all the begging she could into her voice. She leaned forward between the pilots' seats far enough to press a breast against his arm and pawed at his chest. "Please, Vlad. Let me see her fly!"

"*Zroby tse!*" The general commanded with a broad wave of his arm that clipped Manny with a solid punch. "Do it! *Da,* go!" Then he shouted confidentially to Manny, "We shall show both these wenches many fine things tonight."

And Manny began cycling up the helicopter. As soon as the radios blinked to life, he spoke to the general.

"You better tell the tower we're taking it out. So they

don't shoot us down." He said it like the funniest joke in the world and Vlad roared with laughter.

"Yes! Yes! Good idea!"

Then Alisa had another idea and once more held tightly onto the general's arm, "Take us over the water. I want to see the moonlight on the Black Sea. It's *so* romantic, Vlad. Tell them that, too."

And the general did.

"**This is Lieutenant Manfred** Malcolm. Are we a go?"

"Roger that," the Air Mission Commander called out. "We're a go."

"This should be a quick one, if we can trust intel," Manny called back, knowing exactly who had done the background research for the mission.

"Damn straight you can, Mr. Lieutenant Manny!" Mila's tone was teasing as she cut into the radio circuit. Her language had become as rough as his own. It sounded good on her, brash and full of life.

He *knew* he could trust her. Over the last six months she'd proven herself every bit as sharp as she was beautiful.

"And you make it quick. No three-day holiday in Crimea this time. We have wedding tomorrow. I may be single woman going up this aisle, but I will be married woman walking back down this aisle. That, or you will not be walking so good. *Da?*"

"Whatever you say, Duchess." He yanked up on the collective and shoved the cyclic forward to lay the hammer down hard. "On my way."

46

# FLYING OVER THE WAVES

*No one gets shot down during a training mission.*

*Except* **Chief Warrant Officers Debbie Rosenthal and Silvan Exeter.** *Their Little Bird helicopter plummets toward the North Sea during a Force 9 severe gale.*

*With no hope in sight, they must struggle together to survive Flying Over the Waves.*

# INTRODUCTION

This story has a simple origin.

If the 5E is extreme, then they must fly in all conditions. When any other outfit is safely grounded, the Night Stalkers still have a promise to keep to their military customers: Any time, anywhere.

That means they must train to fly in those conditions as well.

In fact, some of the very first Night Stalkers deaths were pilots trying to push the envelope of night flying—before the advent of night-vision goggles. And much of what we possess of NVG gear was initially developed for and *by* the Night Stalkers.

Of course, I couldn't have my elite flyers just…crash.

I needed some extreme cause.

My wife listens to the 150+ year old BBC *Shipping Forecast* just for the fun of it. And when there is a truly horrendous set of storms, she tells me about them. If you want a fascinating read of just how nasty these storms can be, I can highly recommend John

Rousmaniere's *Fastnet, Force 10: the deadliest storm in the history of modern sailing.*

So, I sent my Night Stalkers out into the middle of a gale. But even that wasn't enough to take down a SOAR pilot. *That* took getting shot out of the sky by an overly nervous Russian trawler.

Because it is set in the middle of a gale, it's a story that happens fast, making it one of my shortest romances.

But that wasn't the real challenge for me in this story. The challenge was facing my heritage. Debbie Rosenthal was perhaps the very first Jewish character I tried to write. (Other than the One God in my irreverent romps *Cookbook From Hell: reheated* and *Saviors 101: the first book of the reluctant Messiah.*)

My heritage is 100% Ashkenazi Jew (I'm a rare pure blood in the modern era). But it is also a heritage and a culture that my parents had no interest in. After the age of five, the next time I was in a synagogue was at the age of thirty-five while visiting a historic site in Cochin, India. I am only now, so many years later, starting to discover bits and pieces of my heritage.

And I'm doing that through my characters.

1

"Since when do people get shot down on training missions?"

"At the moment I'm more worried about the North Sea," her copilot shot back.

Night Stalkers Chief Warrant 3 Debbie Rosenthal decided that he had a point.

Tonight the North Sea was being thrashed by a mid-December Force 9 severe gale—that felt like a Force 12 hurricane the way it shook her helicopter. It slammed them around in all three dimensions with the ease of a beach ball. Command had decided that gale force winds in the fifty mile-an-hour range was a good excuse for training.

Debbie hadn't argued.

First off, Command wouldn't care what a mere CW3 said any more than her father had. He'd disowned her the day she'd joined the Army rather than marrying a good Jewish boy.

Second, such an on-the-edge flight fit her own idea of a good skills freshener, well, other than being slammed about the sky. The Night Stalkers of the US Army's 160th SOAR 5th Battalion E Company were tasked with flying their helicopters through every form of ugly and it was great practice—when they weren't shooting at you.

When they weren't *supposed* to be shooting at you.

From a thousand feet up, flying over the North Sea in the middle of the night had merely been a good ride. From a thousand feet up over freezing waves two-to-three stories tall, breaking in huge sheets of slashing spray—with no engine—it was far less amusing.

The external cameras were good enough to paint the picture across the inside of her visor in horrifying detail despite the darkness.

"Are you sure we were shot?" It was a dumb question, but it came out anyway.

Chief Warrant 2 Silvan Exeter just pointed at the hole in their windshield that was currently shooting a stream of cold rainwater between them. The radio and engine had vanished at the same moment as their engine. The miracle was that neither of them had been hurt.

The other Little Bird in their flight hadn't been so lucky, but she couldn't think about Junker and Tank at the moment.

Their two-helicopter flight had passed above a fishing trawler seventy miles off Aberdeen, Scotland. At the time (all of sixty seconds ago) it had seemed like a good idea to do hover practice over a clear reference point. Could they hold position, in formation, directly above the trawler no matter what the wind and waves were doing? The trawler probably wouldn't even know they were there, testing hover skills in the night.

Thirty seconds ago, the trawler had unveiled a Soviet ZU-23mm anti-aircraft gun.

*Not* fishing trawler.

Russian *spy* trawler.

Her aircraft was damaged first. Then the ship had swung fire against the other Little Bird and held it there. The second aircraft had plummeted out of the sky, no attempt at control or recovery. They were swinging back to finish her off as well, but it took too long. By then Silvan had fired a trio of Hydra 70 rockets into the trawler.

Debbie felt the billow of the massive explosion despite the gale-level wind. Everything above sea level was erased—gun, gunner, the entire trawler. In her infrared night vision—which was still working by some miracle—she could see the remains of the hull were awash and would sink soon. Even if it was an act of idiocy, it was also an act of war. There was going to be hell to pay if anyone lived to report it.

There were only two of them left out here in the middle of the North Sea and the odds didn't look good.

Per protocol, Silvan kept calling out the engine restart procedures while going through the emergency checklist…not that anything was likely to work.

Any further disbelief that her subconscious was tossing out upon the waters would have to wait until later. After she didn't die.

Debbie could feel the heavy weight of the wind shuddering through the controls.

No hydraulic assist in a MH-6M Little Bird.

No crew chiefs in back performing some miracle, like fabricating a new engine out of old bullet casings in the sixty seconds she'd be able to keep them aloft. That was the land of Black Hawks and Chinooks. In the Little Bird, it was just the two of them.

Autorotation was dicey at the best of times. Autorotation with winds gusting past fifty and nowhere to land just wasn't going to work.

"Can you reach the raft?"

Silvan hesitated in mid-"Ignition-test on, negative indicators, Ignition-start press and hold, negative start." She'd already lost half her altitude and was descending through five hundred feet. They were at max glide time, minus a factor of extra speed so that the storm didn't flip them too easily. Better faster with less flight time than upside down with only seconds to go. Head-on into the wind to get maximum lift…it didn't matter where they went, so she wasn't worried about distance.

No one ever survived bailing out of a crashing helicopter, so the requirement to carry the small raft on long crossings was silly, but it was on the books. Ditching was something you only survived if balanced perfectly with no rotors catching the water—and in dead calm weather. And then only if you were lucky. Actually, there were survivors during storm ditchings, but they were very rare—more statistical anomaly than fact. A Little Bird wasn't some old-style US Coast Guard HH-3F Pelican designed to float. They were going to sink so fast that hitting the water was barely going to slow them down.

"I can only reach the raft if I go outside," he sounded grim. A Little Bird had a cockpit small enough that Debbie had never understood how two men could fly one. At least her shoulders were narrow enough that they only bumped together half the time they were aloft. The back two seats were even smaller. "Outside" meant stepping out onto the skid, shuffling backward in a roaring wind, and yanking the rear door open—all while she was busy pitching and yawing like a drunkard on a bender.

"Three hundred feet," was the only answer she had for Silvan.

## 2

"Silvan? Like Tolkien's elves? You're tall enough to be one." Debbie leaned back against the nose of her Little Bird, warm in the April afternoon. She looked up at the new guy—six-one, maybe six-two, a long way up. The sun caught his blond hair and made it shine. He was also slender like an elf, except for a very nice set of soldier's shoulders.

"Mom was a fan. And with our last name being Exeter… Exeter College was Tolkien's alma mater. I never stood a chance," new guy shrugged. *Very* nice shoulders. Good smile too. Debbie liked good smiles.

"I didn't know there were elves in the Army. Something's wrong with your ears though."

He fell for it and actually reached up to touch them, before he sighed. "Not pointed. Right. Maybe I'm a deformed elf."

"Or a reformed one." Not one bit deformed from where she was watching. Hide his ears and he'd make a very fair Legolas in the Lord of the Rings movies. His hair was still Army-short, but maybe she could corrupt him. Her own was down to her shoulders. Very un-Army, but very Night Stalkers.

The Night Stalkers' customers—Delta Force especially—let their hair go long to help them blend in when infiltrating undercover. And there wasn't a Delta operator who didn't also glory in the chance to say "up yours" to the military hierarchy that they'd voluntarily sworn to serve to the death. A lot of the fliers in the 160th SOAR took their close association with Delta and SEAL Team 6 as an excuse to let their own hair get long.

"Let it grow out. That'll hide the defect." Because otherwise he was damn near perfect. Not gorgeous, though not homely by a long stretch, but rather cute, strong, and funny. "Besides, you'd look good in long hair."

He squatted down, flexing arms and clenching fists, and grimaced horribly.

"What's wrong?"

He looked like he was holding himself back from pummeling something.

Or maybe trying to give birth right there on the runway in front of her helicopter.

"Is it working?" His voice little more than a grunt.

"Is what working?"

He stopped whatever it was he was doing and patted the top of his head. "Crap!"

"What?"

"A beautiful woman tells me to grow my hair long, I wondered if I could hurry up the process. You know, like the Incredible Hulk." When he resumed the hunched, grimace-riddled stance—she recognized it, right out of the movies.

"An angry roar and you've got it nailed."

And he roared! Right there in the middle of Fort Rucker, Alabama airfield. Other crews were turning startled looks in their direction, but Silvan didn't seem to care.

When he finished, he stood up normally, as if nothing had happened and half the field wasn't watching him, and patted the top of his head again.

Then he whispered a soft, "Damn! No change."

Debbie would have burst out laughing at that moment if she could have, he was awfully cute.

But she couldn't.

Because she knew that in that instant, whether or not she was his commander, she was gone on him.

3

ilvan popped loose his harness then turned
to her.

"Remember, jump into the top of a wave. If you
jump into a trough from a height, you're going to fall
that extra thirty feet."

They were crossing down through the two-hundred-
foot mark and the difference from crest to trough was
looking more like five stories than three. These waves
were huge.

"After I get the raft, we jump together, from opposite
sides," he shouted for emphasis.

"Roger that. Go!"

And he *was* gone: yanking free the data-and-
communications umbilical cord to his helmet, jamming
open the door with a shoulder, then leveraging his way
out onto the bucking skid. The wind roared and swirled
about her for a moment before the wind slammed it
closed.

She should have said something.

Something to show that she cared.

That he was important.

That even though they'd never had a chance, she wished they had.

A vicious gust slapped them hard. She managed to lean her side of the Little Bird into it. It cost her some altitude, but it would spare Silvan the worst of it.

She was way too busy to look to see if he was still there, clinging to the outside of the helo.

One-fifty.

The wind's roar in the cabin returned with double the volume.

The rear door was open. Silvan was still with her.

"I've got the raft!" Debbie could barely hear his shout.

"Keep growing your hair!" *Stupid! Stupid! Stupid!*

*That* was going to be the last thing she ever said to him?

4

"Keep trying," Debbie managed past a constricted throat, trying not to make their first meeting too awkward. "Six months tops and it should cover those awkward ears."

"Mom would like you."

"She doesn't like the kind of trollops you normally drag home?" Maybe it was the Alabama heat shimmering off the airfield that melted what little manners she normally maintained.

Silvan had the decency to laugh despite her catty remark. "Not much. Would you believe that some of them haven't even read *The Hobbit?*"

"Horrors!"

"Indeed," he agreed.

And that had set the tone for their entire first meeting. They'd shared stories of trainings and missions, of joining the military and that they were each nearing their first decade of service.

She'd felt bad about not sharing her past, but Silvan made it easy with stories of his own. His family life wasn't some picture postcard, but it wasn't a dysfunctional TV sitcom either. Engineer mom, professor dad, older sister lawyer with one kid and a divorce.

For eight months they'd flown together, laughed together, and survived every mission thrown at them.

In eight months he'd never done a single thing to reverse her initial impression.

Silvan was a seriously decent guy who easily kept up with her quirky sense of humor. Even better, together they forced each other to become better fliers.

It seemed they'd done everything together —except one.

5

*W*ell, two things. They'd also never died together but, odds on, they were about to.

She didn't dare take a hand off either of the controls, so she couldn't do anything to prepare for the jump except rehearse the steps in her head: release controls, punch harness release with one hand, then yank out the helmet's umbilical cord while opening the door with the other. Thankfully, she and Silvan were already wearing inflatable life vests on top of their standard gear.

With her left thumb she flicked the landing light switch on the end of the collective control. The sudden glare revealed a nightmare landscape of sheeting spray and breaking waves covered with foaming spindrift.

A wave crested fifty feet below her.

No time to grab anything, just enough to—

Down in the trough was what remained of the spy trawler's hull.

A flat structure. The lowest deck had survived the blast. Now just barely awash.

If she could land there, even for a moment, their chances of survival were going to skyrocket.

64

## 6

"Why don't you have a past?"

Debbie sat slouched beside Silvan after a brutally long mission deep into Libya to take part in wiping out an al-Qaeda camp. They'd made it back to the USS *Harry S. Truman* aircraft carrier with the first of the predawn light. By unspoken mutual consent, they'd found a corner of the hangar deck with a view out over the ship's wake. There they'd collapsed and settled in to watch the sunrise over the Mediterranean.

For a long time—from dark blue to soft pink—Debbie just let the waves hold her attention. She felt their beat in her aching body. Little Birds were meant for two-hour out-and-back operations. Muhammad Ali's "Sting like a bee"—that was a Little Bird's sweet spot. Which fit her perfectly, as her full name, Deborah, meant "bee" in Hebrew. Long missions took their toll. Ones long enough to require multiple refueling stops really took the honey right out of her mood.

Silvan waited her out. He was good at that, sensing her mood and letting her have that space. There was so much to appreciate about him aside from his skills as a flier.

"You weren't born the day you joined the Army." He was also good at calling her on her own bullshit avoidance, even if she didn't appreciate it.

"I'm a bad Jewish daughter. I didn't marry a Jew. I didn't even go into business or law. Except my family isn't just Jewish, they're Orthodox Haredi. It means we aren't supposed to even mingle with non-Jewish cultures."

"So the Army ticked them off. Is that why you joined?"

Debbie had to smile, "Can't say that I minded that aspect of it, but no. There was a boy at our *yeshiva*—think Jewish high school that only reluctantly allows girls —Moshe. He was by far the best of us all. But he was in the wrong place at the wrong time—a mugging that escalated badly. Anyway, he was dead before they got him to the hospital. That was the moment I truly became aware of the outside world. The more I learned..." she couldn't finish the sentence.

"The more you felt a need to fix it?"

She could only nod. She didn't even mind Silvan's habit of being able to finish her sentences because he was always right when he did. The waves of her life kept flowing by like the sunlit wake of the aircraft carrier as she watched—no way to ever hold onto them. No way to ever bring them back.

## 7

"Hull!" Debbie shouted as loudly as she could.

By the wind's roar—now augmented by the breaking waves—she knew the rear door was still open and Silvan was still with her.

If he responded, she couldn't hear it. But the roar filled her ears—they'd jump together.

She flew so close above the next crest that she could have stepped out onto the wavetop. A second later, she was over the yawning chasm of a trough. But the hull had survived or at least a piece of it.

Forty.

Thirty.

At twenty she reefed back on the cyclic hard, a final flare to dump speed and trade it in for a momentary, unsustainable hover.

A last kick of the rudder pedals.

Impact!

More of a crash than a landing onto the trawler, but it had worked.

Now all her years of training kicked in.

Not turning to Silvan—not even hesitating to be surprised that she was still alive—she slapped, pulled, opened, and leapt out.

She dove into the freezing sea and slammed against the two feet of the trawler's outer wooden hull, then collapsed onto the flat deck. She ate a mouthful of saltwater as she groaned at the abuse. A glance up revealed the Little Bird's rotors still windmilling at lethal speed.

The next wave began to lift the hull and the helo fell, tipping toward her. Nowhere to dive. Her life vest— which had auto-inflated on contact with the water—kept her pinned to the surface like a bug about to be squashed.

Through the driving sleet and icy spray, she saw the blades slash into the water less than an arm's length past her position. Without the engine driving them, they stopped almost immediately.

She felt like a lion in a carbon-fiber blade cage: the body of her helo behind her and the blades driven down into the sea in front.

Then the wave's face went near enough to vertical for the helicopter to roll off the hull. She actually banged her helmet on some part of the helo as it tumbled by—driving her face once more into the frigid wash of water now two feet deep over the sinking deck. Her helo disappeared beneath the waves.

Just because the boat's hull was wallowing so deeply, didn't abate the wave's vehemence. In a cloud of slashing spray and biting wind, it flipped the hull over this time. Catapulting her aside with the ease of a rag doll, she landed clear of its tumbling mass.

Too much for the remains of the trawler, it finally plunged for the depths. Caught in its vortex rush of sinking water, she was dragged deep beneath the surface.

She swam hard, letting the life vest tell her which way was up and broke the surface just before her lungs burst from holding her breath so hard. She slid down the back of the wave.

A light blinked in the darkness.

Silvan.

Just going over the crest of the next wave over.

He might as well be a mile away.

8

---

$\mathcal{S}$ilvan wiped the water out of his eyes for the hundredth time since he'd plunged into the icy North Sea. Alone, he rode over the wave and down the far side, bobbing as lightly as a cork.

If ever there was a pilot to fly with, it was Chief Warrant Deborah Rosenthal.

Which was exactly how he felt every time he got close to her. He'd like to have gotten much closer, but the Army wasn't the only one against that. Their rank wasn't an issue, but the fact that she was his superior officer was. He hadn't wanted to risk not flying with her in the future.

There was also something within her. Something… torn. It had kept him pushed to a distance and he'd done his best to respect that.

And now he didn't know if he'd ever have a chance to see past whatever that was, or even to thank her for saving him.

Had she died in that final act?

There was no way he should be alive, but she'd been

masterful. Landing for those crucial few seconds on the hull had absolutely saved his life.

He'd felt the skid hit the boat's hull through the heels of his boots. The next instant he had kicked backward as hard as he could, flinging himself clear. With the two-foot-long life raft bag clutched hard to his chest, he hadn't sunk more than a few feet.

Then he'd watched in horror as first the helicopter and then the entire boat hull flipped over on where she would have jumped clear. If she even survived the landing.

He wiped his face again and tried to kick himself in a circle, hoping against hope that he'd spot the light from her life vest.

Night.

Screaming wind.

Pitch-black, overcast night.

Yet, he could see shades of the gale's madness—the waves as they ripped past him.

No thought to grab the night-vision goggles that he kept stowed under the console. When attached to the helicopter, everything he needed was projected on the inside of his visor.

Next time, if there was a next time, he'd remember to grab his goddamn NVGs.

A glimmer?

He watched closely over the next wave crest.

Definitely a brightness beyond the next wave. The only light in the night, he'd take hope from that.

He hooked the uninflated life raft to his belt on a short tether so that it would trail behind him and began swimming.

## 9

Debbie had lost sight of Silvan. No matter how hard she swam, he seemed to slip farther and farther away.

She made sure that her emergency radio beacon was blinking, indicating it was crying for help, but how long was rescue going to take to reach her? She was fifty miles from land in every direction in the midst of a brutal winter storm. The first shot had killed the helo's radios and there'd been no time to try the handhelds.

Now, to hear her little beacon, it would take a very lucky satellite or someone flying directly over her and listening for her signal. How long before Search and Rescue came looking? Too long.

It was just her and Silvan.

No, it was just her.

That thought slammed in with a punch harder than the icy ocean seeping into her foul-weather flight gear. Next time she flew, she'd wear a goddamn dry suit.

No Silvan. She hadn't let him get too close to her because…

A wave crest slapped and tumbled her. Rather than burying her under, the wind ripping at the water was enough to blow her through the air for a short distance and bury her face-first into the water, again. She resurfaced.

Because she was an idiot.

Silvan Exeter was the best man she was never going to meet again. Impossibly, even better than Moshe who had been swept backward by the tide of time as well.

She'd lost all sense of direction when the wave had tossed her.

She treaded water, slowly turning in a circle, searching for any sign of hope. Deborah the Prophetess had led the biblical legions against the oppression of King Jabin and his military general Sisera. The latter had fallen to a woman pounding a tent peg through his temple while he rested. Well, Debbie didn't have a tent peg, a mallet, or the knowledge of a prophetess of the Lord God.

All she had was—

A shining beacon in the distance. A tiny flashing light.

Attached to a man plunging down a wave face easily five stories tall.

As he swam *in her direction.*

A rescue swimmer? Already?

No!

Leaving the chill that had threatened to encase her behind a solid wall, she dug into the waves, speeding toward Silvan.

1 0

---

$\mathscr{B}$oth cold, gasping for breath from the hard swim necessary to fight their way together, and lost in the North Sea—the first thing they had done was kiss.

It had been sloppy, hurried, freezing, and in moments they were battered apart except for the death grip on the front ring of each others' vests.

But it changed Silvan's world.

It hadn't been a kiss of "so glad to see you."

Their coming together had been an "Oh my god, I thought you were dead!"

It took a coordinated effort, but they deployed the raft and managed to climb in before it blew away. It was small comfort in the heavy storm—it didn't stay dry, but at least it remained upright. Between judicious bailing and unfurling the canopy, they finally were reasonably secure.

The only way they could keep from being slammed together was by holding tightly to each other. It was something that Silvan had wanted to do for so long that it was hard to believe it was finally happening. Not how he'd imagined it, but holding her tight might just be the best thing to ever happen to him.

"You aren't going to die!" Debbie shook him by her hold on his vest.

It seemed an odd statement as this was perhaps the safest they'd been in over an hour.

"You aren't!" She shook him again.

"You're awfully strong for someone who isn't an elf."

She shook him again, though not as hard. As if she could anchor her words in his chest.

If they hadn't been deep in the comparative calm inside the high-sided raft, he wouldn't have heard her next statement.

"I'm not wrong this time. I can't be. You're going to live." Then she buried her face against his shoulder and simply hung on.

There, with the waves raging by dozens of feet above them, he knew he had found the missing piece, the tear in her world.

Moshe. He wasn't "some boy" who had died and changed the course of Debbie Rosenthal's life.

She'd been there. Held him while he died, telling him he was going to live. Her boyfriend? Her lover?

"Did he save you?"

Her nod told him the rest of the story. Moshe had died to protect her and she was repaying him by protecting everyone else that she could.

Silvan held her tightly, and she let him.

An eternity of howling winds and bailing out icy seawater later, a big C-130 Hercules turboprop roared by close overhead, soaring through the first light of day. It had sniffed out the track of their emergency locators.

The satellite phone had been useless, the wave troughs too deep to allow even the time to place a call. Their handheld radios were only good for line-of-sight communications. But now with the big plane circling above, he pulled out the radio and told them they were safe and uninjured…and that there was no point searching for the other two pilots. The rest of the report would be for the company commander's ears alone. He could decide who to contact about the spy trawler.

Within the hour, a helo and a rescue swimmer would arrive to hoist them off the waves. The plane promised to stay on station despite the turbulence their crew must be suffering.

Debbie lay quiet now, comfortable inside the circle of Silvan's arms while they awaited the rescue team that would pluck them from the sea. Their helmets kept the worst of the howling wind at bay.

"You don't need to worry about protecting me."

Silvan's shouted words were like a benediction. He might not understand that she hadn't had a single thought of her own survival during the crash landing— she'd been shocked when she'd survived. But she'd known without a doubt that getting down on that hull had improved Silvan's chances of survival. That was all that had mattered.

But maybe he was right. She didn't need to protect him as if he could be erased from existence at any moment. He'd survived the gunfire and crash just as they'd survived dozens of missions.

When it was their time, like Junker and Tank, it would be their time.

Until then—

Debbie sat up as much as the pitching raft would

allow and studied Silvan's face. A few strands of his beautiful blond hair were finally long enough peek out from under the edge of his helmet.

"I've got an idea."

His frown said that he couldn't hear her.

She braced herself against his shoulders by curling her fists around his vest's armholes. Then she leaned in and repeated her shout between his right cheek and the edge of his helmet.

"Bring it on, lady. If it's a good one, I'll put in a good word for you with the elf king." His breath was warm against her chilled cheek.

"How about we just worry about protecting each other?"

"Sounds like a good plan." Then Silvan's face sobered, "How long were you thinking?" He had to repeat that more loudly.

When he did, Debbie couldn't help but feel the warmth in her heart despite the hail and spray currently battering at them. "How long have you got?"

Silvan's easy smile started slow but built big and then disappeared from view when he kissed her to seal the bargain.

Debbie let her heart ride the wave as it lifted the two of them out of the trough and over the top together.

She hoped they had a long, long time.

# SINCE THE FIRST DAY

**Co-pilot Danny Corvo** accepts his role as straight man on the jovial crew aboard the Night Stalkers' helicopter *Calamity Jane II*. Ignoring his attraction to the wildly vivacious **Crew Chief Carmen Parker** proves to be much more difficult.

Racing through the tail end of a hurricane off the Panamanian coast—what a crazy time to declare his feelings.

But this stormy night must be the one to tell her how he's felt Since the First Day.

# INTRODUCTION

Throughout the 5E novels, Danny was always the quiet one. And I was curious as to why.

Carmen, on the other hand, was one of my most vociferous, wise-cracking, take-no-hostages characters. She and Trisha O'Malley… Someday I should write a story where the two of them meet and compare notes. Hmmm…

This story oddly enough came about by accident.

I was writing the third book in my Delta Force series, *Wild Justice,* when Carmen and Danny's Chinook was tasked with delivering my Delta team onto a cruise ship for a takedown practice mission. Carmen was doing her normal acting-out thing…but something went sideways and I wasn't quite sure what it was.

I've learned to listen to those odd quirks that the characters come up with.

First, Carmen was being even more chaotic than usual. And second, why in the world did they start singing "The Sound of Music"?

That's a song that holds a curious importance to me.

Again dating myself, but I was just a kid when that movie came out and I fell in love. I mean she'd been good in *Mary Poppins,* but in *Sound of Music*...OMG! Nothing against my mom, but I *so* wanted Julie Andrews to be my mother.

So, it's kind of an important song for me.

Why had Carmen started singing it in the middle of a Delta Force novel in which she was just a minor character?

And so was born this story.

1

*Present Day, June 13, 2300 Hours (11 p.m. Panama Local Time)*

"It was a dark and stormy night!" Danny Corvo declared over the intercom as he fought the big helo's controls.

"Ho-ly crap!" Carmen's words were jarred out of her by the *Calamity Jane II* slamming into another squall line as if it was a solid wall. "Did Danny just make a jo-ke?"

He should have kept his mouth shut and just flown the damn helicopter.

The massive Chinook twin-rotor helicopter was getting battered by the tail end of a tropical storm they were using for cover on this training mission. The last thing to do under those conditions was to encourage Carmen.

"He did?" "What did I miss?" The other two gunners, probably woken up by Carmen's initial shout, chimed in like it was some special event they didn't want to miss. The Night Stalkers of the 160th Special Operations Aviation Regiment—SOAR—could sleep through almost anything. Except one of Carmen's cheery blasts.

"Do another one, Danny. Do another one," Carmen pleaded like a toddler rather than being a definitely grown up, way hot redhead.

Captain Justin Roberts just grinned over at him from the pilot's seat. *You've stepped in it now,* written clear across what little Danny could see of his face. From the nose up, his features, like Danny's, were covered by his visor and helmet.

It was an odd habit that made them turn to each other for a joke, but not during anything to do with flying. It wasn't as if they could see much. Most of his vision was blocked by the tactical view projected on the inside of his visor. The captain was a pale version of himself set beyond the display.

He would have been invisible if they were over land, but at the moment they were beating ass toward an unsuspecting ship at sea with a team of Delta Force in the back. They had a Zodiac boat and were doing some exercise about taking down a cruise ship. Even storm-whipped, the sea didn't paint much on the tactical display.

Danny refocused on the inside of his visor. The weather was painted in large swaths of "don't go here" lying exactly in their path. Of course they'd just flown through a whole section just like it over the last half hour, so that didn't worry him. The horizon was a pale line across the center of his view with altitude, airspeed, and other critical readouts down the left. Dead ahead lay four symbols for ships: cargo and container carriers whose jobs were not being fun at the moment with the thirty-foot seas. And over the horizon, a small red rectangle pinpointing their target—a disabled luxury cruise liner, empty and under tow. Justin's wife Kara Moretti was back aboard the USS *Peleliu* and had the ship pinpointed for observation with her Gray Eagle drone quietly circling far above.

At least the Delta Force team was on their own circuit, so they'd still be able to sleep. It wasn't like Delta ever spoke to anyone else—ever—anyway. And not even to each other much that he'd seen.

"Please, please, please," Carmen wasn't going to let him go.

"Carmen. Begging. I like it," he took another run at being brave.

A fist thumped down on his shoulder which told him Carmen had shifted forward to the observer seat close behind the side-by-side pilots' seats. She was a very physical gal—which sent his thoughts in entirely the wrong direction. He supposed he was lucky, she'd probably have done it much harder if she'd known where his thoughts went so often.

"Picking on your pilot-in-command. Very dangerous, Carmen. *Picking* on the *PIC*," he emphasized the play on words, too late realizing that was probably too obvious.

"Why dangerous, Danny? It's just you."

"Maybe you're in the mood for a swim." Mission profile said stay low, the storm said stay high, he was a Night Stalker so he'd climbed a hundred feet above the waves, rather than the five thousand any rational Army pilot would have. The Night Stalkers flew at the edge of what he liked to call rational insanity. He'd become very comfortable with that over his five years with the 160th.

"Swim with the dashing Danny Corvo? Be sti-ill my heart." A microburst bounced them up fifty feet before he could compensate. Maybe staying a *little* farther from the waves would be a good idea. He took it as a sign from Mother Nature and stayed where she'd just bounced them to. They'd now be visible from farther away, not that radar would pick them out in this crap. The rain lashed so hard against the windshield and hull at their hundred-and-fifty-mile-an-hour speed, plus an obnoxious amount of wind velocity, that he could hear it despite his helmet. It was louder than the beastly big rotors of his Chinook.

"Swimming with you? That *totally* works for me."

A couple of the guys hooted encouragement. It was rare for anyone to banter with Carmen past the first round or two. Her wit was faster than an RPG and not much less dangerous.

He glanced at the engine readouts, even though that was Justin's job at the moment, with Carmen as a backup. The temperatures looked good, so the rain wasn't enough to drown the twin, five-thousand horsepower Lycoming engines. He turned his attention back to keeping them in the air.

And to picturing Carmen in a dark red bikini that matched her hair. Her fair skin and blue-green eyes the color of the tropical sea. Which at the moment was pitch black because it was almost midnight in a bitch of a storm a hundred-and-sixty miles off Panama. Almost midnight. It was hard to not smile even if it didn't really mean anything, except to him. He checked the dash clock, 2304 and counting.

"No, none of you mugs will *ever* see me in a bikini, so just stop thinking about that."

"Which plants the image firmly in my brain," Danny heaved on the thrust control along the left side of his seat to compensate for a sudden downdraft, but managed to stabilize at eighty feet above the waves before climbing back up.

"Ho-ly crap!" There was no air pocket to jar her words this time, so she did it herself. Damn but she was funny. "You guys heard that? You!" She poked him in the arm. "What did you do with our quiet and shy Danny Corvo?"

"I put him out to pasture where he belongs."

"Whoa!" "You were right, Carm." Vinnie and Raymond chimed in from the back.

"This *is* a passel of strange, ain't it," the captain agreed, his Texan accent far thicker than normal.

Danny liked flying with Justin Roberts. He was always cheery—even when everything was going to hell. Justin also gave him plenty of pilot-in-command time. He'd flown with a lot of commanders who just wanted you to sit your ass in the seat and leave them alone. However, egging Carmen on wasn't going to help anyth—

"Crazy weird," Carmen agreed. "It *sounds* like Danny. And I can see his cute little chin."

Just how every Army Special Operations guy wanted to be described by a hot soldier woman.

"*Where oh where has our Danny gone?*" The captain broke into song as he was apt to do at the drop of his cowboy hat.

Danny did his best to ignore it as they mangled the

verse. At least until Carmen joined in with that sweet alto of hers for the refrain, *"Aliens done took him away."*

Images of sticklike green men bearing rectal probes —and a particularly hard slam by the storm—definitely knocked the bikini-clad redhead out of his thoughts. Too bad. If his imagination was worth shit, she'd be damn cute in one.

2

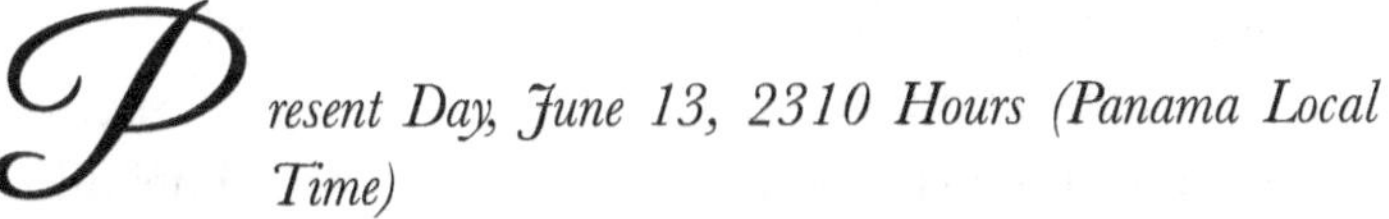

*resent Day, June 13, 2310 Hours (Panama Local Time)*

Danny had never joined in the singing aboard the *Calamity Jane II*. Carmen had teased him about that any number of times, to no avail. At least he'd stopped complaining about their choices of music, mostly.

He was such a quiet guy that he was hard to read. Even his laughs were quiet and his looks thoughtful. Though she could never tell quite what was going on behind those steady eyes.

"Why are you always such a serious guy?" The question was out before she could stop herself.

"Am I? I thought I was a happy-go-lucky leprechaun. Damn, and I was so close to finding me a pot of gold."

"Thought you said you were Portuguese." He looked it with those deep brown eyes, black hair, and sun-dark skin. He was also too handsome for words.

"That was the other Danny Corvo."

The others laughed, but Carmen was actually a little

worried and found it hard to join in. This *wasn't* the Danny that she knew. He wasn't the kind of guy to crack under the stress of a flight no matter how horrid—to emphasize the point, her teeth clacked together sharply as the seat's shocks bottomed out hard in the next air pocket. But she couldn't imagine what was up with him.

She spent a few moments on the HUMS interface— as she'd been doing every five minutes or less of their ride through the storm. The helo's Health and Usage Monitoring Systems was reporting no problems, though she often *heard* problems before HUMS reported them. After nine years in Chinooks, the last two as a Night Stalker crew chief, the aircraft was in her blood. And no matter what the pilots thought, this was *her* bird. She was responsible for every nut, bolt, and signoff. The pilots just climbed aboard on occasion to do some flying.

She rested her hand against the inside of the hull and could feel it vibrating with the controlled violence of the twin Lycoming turbines spinning at fifteen thousand RPM and the uncontrolled violence of the storm. She could also feel every little shift in attitude and speed. It was unreal how fast Danny compensated for everything the storm could throw at him. Maybe he *was* some alternate version of himself.

For a while she simply rode along, enjoying the connection between them. The motion of the helo tied to the constant tiny corrections Danny made on the cyclic and thrust control. She couldn't see his feet on the rudder pedals in the dim light, but she could imagine the expert dance he used to keep fifteen tons of helicopter and crew headed toward their destination.

But she couldn't explain the sudden surfacing of a sense of humor. She liked knowing exactly what was going on with *all* of her equipment, and having a copilot suddenly develop a sense of humor was definitely throwing her.

Not that Danny was *hers*. He was actually the only one on the crew who hadn't at least made a pass at her. Of course Justin's had been after he was happily married to the lethal Kara Moretti, so it had been pure tease that she'd happily returned in kind.

But for her there'd always been something special about Danny.

She remembered her first day as a Night Stalker... which had been a night much like this one.

3

_T_wo _Years Ago, June 14, 2320 Hours (Alabama Local Time)_

The downgraded hurricane had been beating the shit out of southern Alabama as a tropical storm when she'd gotten off the plane at Fort Rucker. It was a real "sicker" of a flight, everyone who wasn't a seasoned flier had been puking their guts out for the entire second half. Even some of the old hands lost it just from listening to all the others.

Carmen would admit that she'd regretted the gut bomb bacon-cheeseburger she'd had just before flight, but refused to be humiliated by seeing it again quite so soon.

She was a Night Stalker crew chief—at long last Fully Mission Qualified. And FMQ Night Stalkers didn't lose their shit because of a little lumpy air. Nonetheless glad to be on the ground, she shouldered her duffle, yanked on her helmet against the last of the six new inches of rain Alabama had gotten that day, and stepped off the flight squarely into a seriously handsome man's chest.

She flattened him right onto his ass.

"Boy, you sure are a pushover," she managed to keep her feet, barely. The rest of the flight began unloading to either side of them as the man she'd plowed into continued to lay in a puddle on the tarmac looking up at her. The storm cracked with lightning, revealing his bewildered expression, as fast-following thunder said the latest weather wasn't done with them yet.

"Sergeant Carmen Parker?"

She nodded and offered a hand, not that she was all that steady yet from the rough flight, but it seemed the least she could do.

He shook his head, either trying to clear it or to say no.

But before she could withdraw her hand, he'd taken it and let her help him to his feet.

"Thanks."

"This is your definition of personal space?" The man stood just inches away, their clasped hands the only thing keeping them apart. So close that it was hard to tell, even in the light spilling out of a nearby hangar, if he was really as handsome as her first impression.

"Not really," he took a step back, then another. He was mighty slow about letting go of her hand though, which was kind of sweet. No complaints from her: muscled, Latino, five-ten to her five-six, and one of those guys who was surprisingly handsome but probably didn't realize it. His easy smile lit his face without doing anything more than saying, "Hi!" No "Hey, baby!" or "Nice to meet you, hot stuff!"

She'd never minded guys flirting with her—

especially because she could kick the ass of anyone who overstepped the bounds. But Danny was like the perfect straight man for her teasing. Maybe even too straight because it didn't seem to phase him in the slightest.

"I'm Danny Corvo, the copilot on your new assignment." Then he shook the hand he'd still been holding and let go. One more step back and "proper personal space" was reestablished.

"Lead on and I will follow," she put a lot of sass into it just to test him.

"This way," he waved toward an electric golf cart of all things. Truly a straight man, unless he was gay. No, she'd seen where his eyes had traveled, however briefly. Then he turned and she saw that he was soaked from butt to brain because of his dunk in the puddle. Yet he made no complaints, no tease. Not even a decent grumble. Weird.

4

---

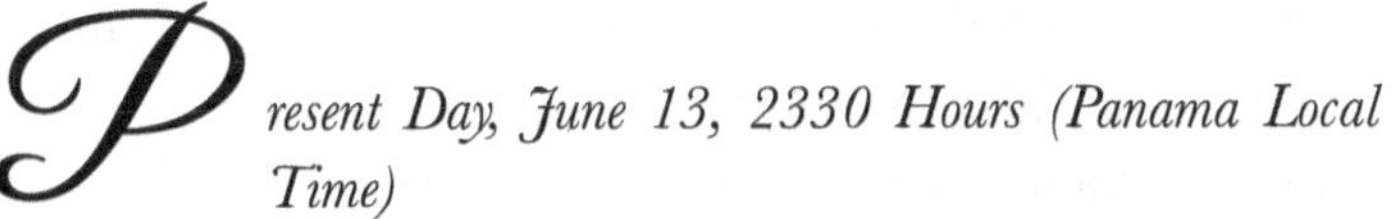

*resent Day, June 13, 2330 Hours (Panama Local Time)*

Even after two years, Danny never quite understood what had hit him that day. The shock of Carmen striding down the flight's ramp like she owned Fort Rucker had been visceral. When she'd slammed into him it had become physical as well. He'd had no extra attention span to even try to recover—he'd simply toppled over.

He'd looked up at the vision of Woman standing over him. Serious curves under a black t-shirt and camo pants. The finer qualities of her figure only emphasized by the heavy duffle she wore backpack-style, pulling her shoulders back. Topped off by a Night Stalkers helmet painted with a flamenco dancer in a flirty red skirt on the side.

Carmen from the opera by Bizet.

It had unquestionably been the new crew member he'd come to fetch from the transport flight, but all he'd been able to do was lie in the puddle and stare as she sassed him.

*Real smooth.*

In two years, he also hadn't figured out what he should have done differently. You didn't just grab a woman like Carmen Parker, her inner strength showed as clearly as her figure from the first moment. In the way she walked, in the way she carried herself, in the way she held focus on what mattered to the exclusion of all else. If she had to walk out into a hail of gunfire to help an injured aboard, she did it without a cringe. If some meathead tried to grab her, she laid him out flat, then dusted her hands of him and went back to whatever she'd been doing. Nothing touched her when turned on that laser focus—which was pretty much all the time.

A particularly heavy squall line in the storm had him climbing up to five hundred feet before they hit it. Sure enough, the solid wall of water that this tropical storm called "rain" took ten percent out of his engines—water just didn't burn very well no matter how much Jet-A fuel you let loose with the throttle.

He kept an eye on the engines as he came out the other side. The Lycomings only took a few seconds to clear their throats and climb back to full power. Damn but he loved this bird. Almost as much as he loved—

Useless thought. Carmen Parker wasn't for the likes of him.

But he couldn't think of anything other than her strength. And her boundless joy and humor—she was funny enough for any five other people combined. That was one of the main reasons he kept his mouth shut. Anything he came up with was going to sound lame next to the cool shit Carmen could deliver on no notice.

Once the engine temperatures had restabilized at fifteen-hundred degrees, he descended back onto profile. Their target ship was well out of the storm now, shifting into the calmer waters close under Panama's mountainous coastline, but he angled in a little deeper into the storm to get them as close as possible while under its cover. Night Stalkers method: push every training opportunity to the limit and maybe, just maybe, you'll have the chance to survive the real thing.

Danny remembered the day things had changed between them. It had nothing to do with mud puddles that had almost earned him a "Danny the Duck" nickname or his soaking flightsuit.

At least not one soaked with water.

5

*One year ago, June 13, 2340 Hours (Yemen Local Time)*
Justin was flying right-seat as usual. But a new copilot flew in Danny's seat—out for an indoctrination run. He was FMQ in the tiny MH-6M Little Bird helicopters. A Little Bird had four seats, but you didn't want to be one of the folks in the back seat, compared to the fifty-plus troops that his Chinook could carry in addition to her five crew. Weighing in at less than a ton apiece, a Chinook could lift fifteen Little Birds without breaking a sweat. But the company commander wanted every one of their pilots to at least have a feel for the capabilities of each airframe type that SOAR flew. And what Pete Napier ordered, nobody messed with.

So, while the copilot had stretched his flight legs over the nighttime Gulf of Aden, Danny had been relegated to the back to see what the crew chiefs did for a living.

"We do all kinds of cool shit back here," Carmen had set them to Intercom Channel 4 so that they wouldn't bother anyone else as she gave him the tour.

"Such as?"

She pointed to Vinnie and Raymond sacked out on the hard steel deck.

"You sleep?"

"You guys up there are just giving us a rocking cradle ride—"

The trainee was slamming the Chinook through a turn worthy of an F-35 Lightning II fighter jet, forcing both of them to hang on so that they didn't tumble about the cargo bay like pinballs.

"No hostiles around," Carmen didn't even break her speech as the helo slid to a halt in mid-air and did a full spin—not an easy trick in a Chinook, which he flubbed the first couple times. "No gunnery practice to do. We might as well grab some shuteye back here. I can run this whole sweet bird by myself."

"Except for flying it," Danny tried to carve out some territory for his role.

"Pilots! Feh!" Carmen wiggled her fingers at him. Then she started guiding him through an in-flight systems check. Every five minutes this, every ten that, and a full tour of the bird's interior along with a dozen systems checks every half hour. She waved the checklists at him, though it was clear she didn't need them. They were at least as long as the pilot's set. "Then when we're on the ground…" she'd pulled out an even bigger set of checklists.

Carmen had always humbled him. Now he was discovering that she was more daunting than he'd thought. If he could just somehow—

"Alert Status One! Alert Status One!" slammed in over the primary intercom channel. Vinnie and Raymond bolted to their feet as if electroshocked.

"You!" Carmen had jabbed a finger against his arm. "You stay attached to my hip or you'll get run over."

"I should—" he pointed forward, but knew he wasn't needed. All through Carmen's tour he'd been aware of the rapidly growing competence of the new pilot as Justin ran him through the paces. A Chinook was no Black Hawk and trading positions in mid-flight was actually possible. But Justin didn't call him forward and he supposed he agreed. Nothing like being at the helm during action to really learn what it took. And Justin Roberts could handle almost anything solo if he had to.

Their little training sortie became a crash-priority evac for a mixed team of the 75th Rangers and Delta. By the time they hit the Yemeni shoreline, a heavily-armed DAP Black Hawk and a Combat Search and Rescue Hawk had joined them as well.

Carmen and Vinnie each shot a few test rounds out of their side-facing miniguns then began checking their personal weapons. He did the same. Raymond went to the rear of the cargo bay and began rigging his ramp gun, even though the ramp was still closed tightly, shutting out the night.

They came in on the terrorist camp low and fast.

Danny presently had the crews' tactical feed on his visor rather than his normal pilot's version. Far more information about the engines and systems performance —next to nothing about the terrain except in the broadest strokes. The threat monitors were soon piecing together the situation. Small arms fire raking along the ground in a vast, back-and-forth interplay of flying death.

The DAP Hawk climbed above the camp and answered back hard.

It was so disorienting when their missile slammed down on one of the compounds—he hadn't known it was coming like he normally would have.

The DAP Hawk gun platform was raining down hell. The CSAR bird was hanging back in case it was needed, and their Chinook was head-on into the fray. On the ground, one Black Hawk was burning fiercely and another was being protected by more soldiers than the one bird could carry out. No…soldiers and several rescued hostages.

Justin—Danny could feel the familiar flight control of the captain taking control—eased the *Calamity Jane II* toward the men on the ground surrounding the beleaguered Black Hawk.

More and more of the fire was directed upward at the DAP Hawk dancing and spinning overhead, which eased the burden here on the ground. Justin got them landed close beside the waiting troops.

The instant the ramp was down, troops stormed aboard. Not all of them were soldiers. Three hostages, two clearly American and the third sounding Japanese, looked battered, confused, and disbelieving at their sudden rescue. There were no hostiles as prisoners. Some operations just didn't call for that.

Several soldiers came aboard with a rifle in one hand and an arm over a buddy's shoulders. Most of those hit the relative safety of the cargo bay and collapsed.

Carmen's station was on the side away from the action—whereas Vinnie's side gun was unleashing a near constant roar of four thousand rounds a minute—

so the two of them grabbed med kits and began helping the worst of the wounded.

The hull rattled with small arms fire. Sometimes a double-smack as a bullet penetrated one side and splatted against the other. Soldiers were hitting the deck as the windows were shot out.

He'd strapped off two legs with tight bandages and was pressing down on a shoulder wound as they lifted. Less than twenty feet in the air, the helo…flinched. Forty thousand pounds of helo wasn't supposed to flinch.

Critical system failure or—

"Corvo!" Justin's voice called him forward. But if he let go on this guy's wound, he'd bleed out before anyone else could get to him.

"You!" Danny shouted a nearby soldier. "Pressure! Here!"

The man was injured himself. "Can't you get the medic?"

Danny tapped the downed man's armband—a red cross bathed in blood. "He *is* your medic."

The guy looked positively green, but placed his hands onto the wounded medic's shoulder.

"If you're gonna be sick, turn to the side so that you aren't sick on him." Then Danny scrambled forward over the bodies of both the wounded and exhausted. The helo was wavering, making him stagger like a drunk on his way forward.

There was no question about what the problem was when he got to the front. The forward windscreen was shattered and the trainee copilot hung limply in his harness.

"Carmen!" Danny shouted out and hoped they still had their private intercom set up.

"Can't see shit!" Justin complained.

Danny saw why. There was blood trickling down his face and it had covered both his eyes. It wasn't gushing, but it wasn't good. The captain couldn't wipe it away because he needed both hands on the controls.

In moments Carmen was at his shoulder.

He gave the blinded Justin moment-by-moment directions on the flight controls while Carmen helped him lever the trainee out of the copilot's seat. He tried not to be too squeamish as he slid in to sit in another man's blood. Finally buckled into the seat's harness, he shouted out, "I have control."

Justin slumped down—having kept them aloft and steady on sheer nerve—and cursed. "Hell of a way to run a rodeo."

Danny flipped to the pilot's view and the full tactical hell of the situation slammed in. Much of the camp was burning. Men were down everywhere, though he didn't see any American bodies—no telltale infrared tabs that would have glowed like searchlights in his night-vision display.

Three soldiers ran from the second Black Hawk— now also burning brightly—toward the back of the Chinook. Danny eased the tail back down. One stumbled and fell—and didn't get up.

From the copilot's raised seat, he spotted the problem. Someone had picked up an AK-47 from a fallen Yemeni and shot the Delta Force operator at least a dozen times from behind, mostly in the leg.

Danny snapped the position lock on the thrust control to free up his left hand. Yanking out his Glock sidearm, he shot twice. Once to blow out his side window, and once to shoot the Yemeni with the AK-47 in the heart.

The shooter collapsed.

Danny slapped the sidearm back in his holster and began easing back down for the wounded Delta.

"CSAR 1. We've got him," a woman's voice. Someone jumped out of the medevac bird and rushed over to the fallen soldier crawling along and dragging one leg.

"Roger. *Calamity Jane II* aloft."

He pulled up and back to clear the CSAR bird and the two grounded and burning Black Hawks. Then got them the hell out of Dodge as soon as the CSAR bird was aloft.

As he was pulling away, he finally got perspective on the shooter he'd just downed and the man he'd taken the AK-47 from in the first place. The shooter was half the size of the dead man.

"I just shot a kid." Probably dropped him on his dad's body.

Carmen, who'd been treating Justin now collapsed in his seat, spun to face him.

He remembered the feel of her comforting hand on his shoulder for a long time after she'd turned back to bandaging the captain.

No one else had heard. He also left that part out of the after-action debriefing.

6

───────────

*P*resent Day, June 13, 2350 Hours (Panama Local Time)

Carmen did a full inspection and systems check as Danny continued to fight them through the storm. A couple of the Deltas were awake. It was a strange team. Three women, four men. She'd never seen a female Delta before and here was a whole clump of them. A gaggle of geese. A flock of ewes. An incoming disaster of Deltas? What would it be like to be a woman who kicked butt at a Delta level? She'd miss her Chinook too much, but the three women looked beyond cool.

One of the guy Deltas called her over.

"Oh. My. God!" Carmen slapped a hand to her chest and put her wrist to her forehead. "I'm gonna faint. It only took four hours for one of the silent warriors to acknowledge that they weren't the only people on this flight." Then she collapsed onto one of the Zodiac's pontoons and fell upside down into the bottom of the boat to sprawl at his feet.

Several of the Deltas startled awake, inspected her strangely for a moment, then went back to sleep.

"Got a question for you, once you're done playing the lead role from a Bizet opera."

"What are you talking about?" She continued laying upside down, but raised her head to inspect him. He was handsome, but she was feeling oddly self-conscious about teasing him, which wasn't like her. She teased everybody—except Danny since that night he'd shot the kid.

"The opera *Carmen.* The dazzling man killer."

"There's an opera named after me?" As if she didn't have Carmen the gypsy dancer emblazoned on the side of her helmet. "How cool is that? Dazzling man killer—perfect fit. Are you my next victim? This should be fun."

The guy looked at his watch, typical Delta.

She flipped around until she was upright once again.

"How would you take down a cruise ship?"

Delta operators had no sense of humor.

"Couple-a Hellfire missiles at the waterline?"

The discussion went on for a few minutes, but her thoughts were on why Danny was acting so strangely. She left the Deltas sitting in their rubber boat in the cargo bay talking about it and drifted back forward.

She ended up close behind the two pilots' seats. She didn't usually ride in the observer's chair, but the memory of the two storms—the present one and the one in which she'd met Danny—had drawn her back to the front.

Her last two years aboard the *Calamity Jane II* stood out so much more clearly than the five prior years in the regular Army or the two years of additional training to become a Night Stalker.

No, that wasn't all of it. Each moment *with Danny* stood out. The good and the bad. The smooth perfection of how he'd flown them out of that battle, despite a windshield so star-cracked that he could only fly by peaking out of the bullet holes marking where unfriendly fire had wounded the captain and killed the last person in that seat, despite the shot-up hydraulics that had forced him to wrestle the massive helo by brute force, all while having just shot a kid. The quiet ease with which he sat back at a hangar barbeque: beer in his hand, smile on his face, just watching the goings on, watching her…

Watching *her*.

With the same look as the moment she'd plowed him ass over teakettle into a mud puddle. A look she'd never forgotten, but couldn't understand. Unless…

Her throat was suddenly dry.

She leaned forward and rested a hand on his shoulder.

He flipped to Intercom Channel 4. One, she finally realized, that they'd shared often for privacy. Privacy? They were just on the same crew together, why did they need a private channel? Yet they had one. Sometimes back-enders (her and the other two crew chiefs) shared Channel 2 so as not to disturb the pilots, but usually the whole team stayed on Channel 1. Danny was the only one she had a "private" channel with.

He waited for her in silence as he held tight control of the bucking bronc that was the Chinook in the storm.

"Danny?"

"Carmen," his voice was "normal" Danny. Not substitute Danny Corvo. No joke or humor. Once again her straight man was there.

"Why…" she couldn't quite bring herself to confront her question directly. "…why don't you ever sing?"

He chuckled with the warmth of a caress, accepting the evasion. "Tone deaf. I've been told that I sing like a choking hyena."

"You can't be that bad."

"Sadly, sometime when we're alone, I can prove it. Besides, if I don't sing it lets me hear you better."

And now they were back to the inexplicable attack of nerves she was having. She checked the HUMS again, but the helo's health was just fine despite the thrashing of the wind and rain. It was hers that was in doubt.

"You're still wondering what I did with the real Danny Corvo?"

"Well…" Carmen took a deep breath and plunged in. "You've always been the straight man. Mr. AJ Squared Away."

"That's sailor talk. What would that be in Army-speak? Mr. Shiny Shithook pilot?" A shithook was slang for an Army Chinook helicopter.

"See! That! That isn't the Danny I know."

"But it is," he whispered as she watched him slew their Chinook around a particularly dense cloud that blanketed a whole section of the radar screen. It was so strange to be having this conversation while he was busy and Captain Roberts was sitting about a foot away, oblivious to everything.

"How? The Danny Corvo I know doesn't joke or tease or—"

"Okay. No tease. There's this beach I know, just down from my grandfather's house, called Praia da

Marinha, in southern Portugal on the Atlantic. Just a few hundred kilometers from where the opera about you is set. Warm. Soft sand with tall cliffs, sea arches, caves. It is one of the most beautiful places I've ever been. I would take you there. Maybe you'd wear a red bikini. Same color as your beautiful hair."

"Already said, no bikini." It was lame, but it was the best defense she had against such a beautiful vision.

"How about a flamenco dancer's dress?"

She sat back and glared at the side of his helmet. That didn't sound like Danny either—no matter how much she liked the sound of it. Her and Danny off somewhere sunny. They'd—

*Her and Danny?*

Her personal HUMS system should be flashing red lights and alert sirens.

"Why didn't you ever say any of this before?" She wanted to grab and shake him. Would have if he wasn't flying.

"Tired of waiting."

"For me?"

"No, me. To be brave."

She wasn't sure if she'd ever met a braver man. Heavy gunfire, his captain wounded, rattled because he'd shot an underage terrorist, and *then* started to re-land his helo to retrieve the wounded Delta. "What in the world do you have trouble being brave about?"

"Not yet."

"What do you mean, not yet?"

"Two more minutes."

She glanced at the mission clock on the helo's main console.

2358.

Too stubborn and maybe too unnerved to ask why, she folded her arms and waited in silence.

She could feel Danny smiling as he flew. They reached the edge of the storm closest to the cruise ship where the Delta operators would soon be simulating an attack. He banked hard, out of the interminable pounding of the storm and into clear air. The wind calmed and even the sky above began clearing as they raced away from the storm. He slid back down toward the sea.

They were the two longest minutes of her life.

It finally flipped to four zeros.

"A new day. Now give."

"Not just any day."

"Danny…" she knew she was grinding her teeth.

"June Fourteenth." He waited.

She didn't get it.

"Two years ago today…"

The date was ringing a bell. It was…the day she'd joined the crew of *Calamity Jane II*. It was the second anniversary of… "Oh shit!"

"Yep! Two years ago you bowled me over and I've never recovered."

"Two years," she could barely breathe.

"It's our second collision-anniversary."

"What was the first?" And then she knew and was sorry she'd asked.

"The kid."

She'd made a point of tracking Danny down afterward at the carrier. He'd been sitting on an old tire in a back corner of the hangar deck, just staring out at the dark sea. She didn't remember what they'd talked about, not much of anything. But they'd sat for hours and she remembered his brief hug and his whispered "Thanks" when the sun rose over the Gulf of Aden.

Again his silent patience while she processed things. He understood her. Everyone else she'd been able to brush off with a joke or a flirt.

Not Danny.

He'd stuck by her. Encouraged her. Made sure she knew she was welcome from that first day. In the Night Stalkers you didn't need someone to push you to excel, everyone did that. Everyone set their standards so high that you just wanted to strive to keep up with them. She was no different. Nor was Danny.

One of the Delta couples came up with a change in the deployment for the exercise. They ran it by her and the two pilots. They'd decided to add a maneuver to the simulated attack.

After she told them it was technically possible— though she kept to herself that it was bat-shit crazy, making it perfect for Delta—they cleared the last of the details with Danny before returning to the cargo bay.

Danny had been her quiet place. Somehow he let her know that she was okay even when she was too tired to speak or too sick of the unending supply of terrorist nut jobs.

He was...the man she didn't know how to live without. When she'd hauled the trainee pilot's body out of the copilot seat, she'd only been able to be thankful that he'd been sitting there rather than Danny. It was a guilty thought, but it ran deep. She would step in front of the bullet herself if it made sure he was still in the world afterward.

"Fifteen minutes to target," Danny announced on the PA.

No response. She turned, and could see that the Delta operators were completing their final prep. Silent warriors indeed.

Danny had stayed silent about his attraction to her. So carefully silent that she'd assumed he wasn't attracted at all, making her keep her own mouth shut about how much she'd been attracted to him. Shut enough that she'd almost buried the feeling. Just kept on being Carmen—wild, funny, in your face.

But now she knew, now she understood that smile on Danny's face. He always laughed with her jokes, but he also saw the quiet person inside her too. It wasn't Carmen the flashy gypsy dancer he was attracted to. It was Carmen Parker, lead crew chief of the Night Stalkers' Chinook *Calamity Jane II*.

"Danny?"

"Carmen," he said it exactly the way he had before.

"You really feel that way?" Was if even possible she could be so lucky?

He twisted all the way around to look at her for just a brief moment. "Really."

She wished she could see his eyes behind the visor, but she could see his smile, and that was enough. With Danny Corvo that was everything and it always would be.

He turned back to flying and she hustled back to make sure the Delta team was ready for the drop. She lowered the rear ramp and peeked out into the night.

The sea was calm, twenty minutes and sixty miles from the storm's closest approach.

The sky was clear.

All the flying ahead wouldn't be smooth. There'd be

more gut wrenchers, but she knew, she just *knew* that they'd get through it all together.

Justin started humming a song over the intercom. Vinnie picked it up with his low baritone and she found herself joining in on the melody before she caught herself.

"What the hell?"

"Y'all amaze me," Justin Roberts spoke over the intercom, his Texas cranked up to full mud-thick. "Like y'all think that simply going up to little old Intercom 4 makes you private somehow. Rest of us tumbled to that trick about six months back. Let me just say, 'bout time, you two." And then he swung back into the music.

"Does this mean I'm going to have to buy a goddamn bikini?"

There was a mass chorus of, "Yes!" without breaking the rhythm.

"Then all you boys are buying goddamn thongs. Beach wedding."

There were laughs over the channel.

"Love you, gypsy dancer. Since the first day," Danny slipped in quietly between the words.

And he was right. "Since the first day," she echoed back.

Then, as she helped the Delta operators launch their boat out into the night, she joined in the chorus.

*The hills (skies,* Danny stuck in) *are alive, with the sound of music.*

"They were right you know," she whispered between the words. "You do sing like a choking hyena."

He only sang louder.

It took an entire chorus before she could stop laughing with joy and join back in.

# THE CHRISTMAS LIGHTS OBJECTIVE

***Kelsey "Killjoy" Killaney*** *can track down the worst drug lord of a Mexican cartel. But of all stupid days, why must it be on Christmas? Her least favorite day of the year.*

***Jason Gould*** *flies with the very best, the Night Stalkers 5E helicopter company. Christmas ranked as his best day every year, until this one.*

*When the mission comes to take out a drug lord on Christmas Eve, maybe they can both track the Christmas Lights Objective.*

## INTRODUCTION

This is another story that has a very personal origin.

I'm not a Grinch by any means, but Christmas as a kid just wasn't a fun time in our household growing up. We were well enough off and the presents were very cool. But between Dad's rants over the bother of the Christmas tree, his mother's imprecations of vile doom for forsaking *her* father's faith (a rabbi back in the old country, not that she kept up any of the Jewish traditions either), and my own mom's joy in a green tree with pretty lights and ornaments… Let's just say that by its very nature, a Jewish household can be very angsty place.

Further, Christmas was when we'd go visit my father's parents in Florida. Flying down from mid-winter in New York, Florida felt so splendidly warm that they couldn't force my sister and I into anything heavier than shorts and t-shirts. Which meant that in the wintry 40s-to-low 50s temperatures we caught horrendous colds every year as a Christmas bonus.

Once I was out on my own, I did my best to avoid Christmas in any manner, shape, or form…for years.

And then I met my wife.

She has the ability to make anything into a quest for joy. And she and my stepdaughter set out to convince me *that* was what Christmas was all about.

They were *very* persuasive. It is now one of my favorite seasons of the year.

So, I took those two opposing forces: Christmas Grouch (not quite Grinch), and Christmas maniac! There were my characters.

But this was the Night Stalkers 5E.

What better than a place that is known specifically for its Christmas lights madness…and for its evil drug lords.

"This sounds as much fun as an air raid at Christmas… Wait, that's what it is." The guy in the goofy Santa hat cut Kelsey off after her opening line of the mission briefing: *This mission flies tonight.*

"Dashing through the air," the senior crew chief of the Night Stalker Chinook helicopter team began singing in her bright soprano. "In a two-rotor heli-sleigh."

"Over the jungle we go, a-fighting all the way," another joined in—an off-key tenor.

The various members of the operation's primary helicopter crew began adding in verses. Soon both pilots and three crew chiefs were rocking to the beat just as if they were in their massive, twin-rotor Chinook.

Sergeant Jason Gould—loadmaster on the *Calamity Jane II* and the man wearing the goofy Santa hat—joined in with a rich baritone. She didn't know why she should be surprised.

But she *was* surprised. He looked like a New York

Jew from her own Brooklyn neighborhood. His speaking voice, while pleasant in the few words she'd been willing to exchange with someone in a Santa hat, hadn't foreshadowed the bone-melting baritone that quickly became the anchor of the song.

She could almost like him, except his hat sported a blinking-nose Rudolph on it. In her book, it was a target saying, "Please shoot me here." Though since they'd just met, and they were both US Special Operations, she left her sidearm in its holster.

They sat in a meeting room in the team's residence building. It stood beside a large hangar—labeled as abandoned. Abandoned deep in the woods of Fort Rucker, Alabama. She'd been directed down a tiny access road that was marked as closed and had looked disused. The gray afternoon, dripping with December rain, made both the building and hangar appear even more sad and weather-beaten. She'd almost turned around—until she noticed the cutting-edge surveillance and security system tucked in the corners of the structures.

The inside of the residence, once she'd gained admittance, was immaculate and comfortable with all of the latest conveniences. She hadn't seen the inside of the hangar yet.

The meeting room's walls were covered in brilliant travel posters—so many of them that they were starting to overlap: Costa Rica, Honduras, and Venezuela were understandable. But there was also Afghanistan, Iraq, Somalia, Libya…

It was the strangest briefing room décor Kelsey Killaney had ever worked in.

"It's my Christmas, too. Not my call." She grimaced as her protest cut off the singing. *Killjoy Killaney.* Once again, the old high school nickname was definitely her. If it *had* been up to her, she'd have scheduled the flight for Christmas Eve anyway, just so that she didn't have to think about "the happy season" for one more millisecond than necessary. But it had been circumstances, not orders that had brought them together on Christmas Eve afternoon.

This morning, everyone at her office in Fort Belvoir, Virginia had been buzzing with the "Best Wishes" and merry yeah-whatever. She'd wanted to lie on the floor and throw a tantrum as if she was nine, not twenty-nine —the little girl wanting everyone to just shut up. Her worldview was more mature now. Now, she was a grown woman who just wished everyone would go away.

Another Christmas wish gone bust. Not that any of the ones as a child had paid off.

This morning, Michael Gibson, the commander of Delta Force, had appeared at her desk inside The Activity's headquarters without warning—not even from security who were there to make sure such things didn't happen. The Intelligence Support Activity worked in one of the most secure buildings on a fort made up of twenty major intel agencies. The Activity's sole purpose was serving the Special Operations Forces, but that didn't mean they were supposed to be able to just walk in.

"There's a jet waiting for you at Davison Army Airfield," had been his idea of a pleasant Christmas Eve morning greeting—which actually worked for her. "Here's your team and mission file to read on the flight."

He'd handed her a slim folder that she wanted to handle as much as a live snake. It had a yellow fly sheet with a dark red border. In large type it only had an identification number and two of the scariest words in the intelligence business: Eyes Only. She'd checked the back of the fly sheet. Her name had been added in the second position, countersigned by Colonel Michael Gibson himself. Theirs were the only two names on the file.

She'd looked back up at him, but he'd been gone. If not for the file clutched in her white-knuckled fingers, she'd have doubted he'd ever been there. One look at the first page and she was on the move. On her way out the door to grab the scram kit from the trunk of her car, she'd stopped off at the front desk. Just as she suspected, he never *had* been signed in…or even seen—Delta Force guys were just creepy sometimes.

Reading the mission portion of the file Gibson had given her, made her the obvious choice for the operation. Actually, the only choice.

Reading the portion about the 5E was just…headshaking.

The 5E had an unprecedented number of missions with an unlikely success rate—even by the Night Stalkers' stratospheric standards. Yet the details of most of their missions had been redacted from the file now sitting in the locked briefcase at her feet.

With their song cut off, they were all sitting and waiting. Waiting and ready for their latest mission assignment. That's when she looked at the posters again.

"Duh!"

Jason, happy in his Santa hat, looked over but she

just shook her head to ward him off. She hoped he would look away before she was forced to attack Rudolph's blinking nose. The last thing she needed was to explain herself to a Night Stalking Christmas elf, no matter how nice a voice he had. Why was a New York Jew singing Christmas carols anyway?

Except he wasn't a fellow Brooklynite. According to the file, Loadmaster Jason Gould was from Florida no matter how much he sounded New York.

Kelsey understood now. She didn't need the list of redacted missions—they were right there on the walls. These people collected travel posters of everywhere they'd ever had an operation. Now she could start putting some of the pieces together.

Each poster was a snapshot of a mission file.

"Find Beauty in Honduras." A black ops Honduran mission last year that had shaken the corrupt banking-military cooperative to the core. It had significantly stabilized the duly-elected government—but no hint of who had done the mission. The answer sat in this room.

"Surf Kamchatka." The 5E had done the Russian drone mission.

"Hike the Negev." The disastrous Negev Desert, Israel, mission that had shaken The Activity itself to the core, somehow salvaged by the field team. By this team.

She tried to catch her breath, but wasn't having much luck. No wonder she hadn't heard of the 5E, though they were the logical extension of Henderson's and Beale's D Company. The 5D had been hugely innovative in their approach to military tactics. The 5E, however, were the tactical equivalent of Delta Force— silent and dangerous as hell…or Christmas.

"Damn it!" Jason complained. "Christmas Eve! Shit, man! And I was going to get my nails done tonight." That earned a laugh around the table. The team was apparently unflappable.

Despite her clumsiest efforts, their spirits remained high.

She got along with data, not people.

Activity agents were rarely in on the final mission. They might go out into the field a dozen times themselves gathering intelligence, but operations were generally left to the action teams. But tonight there was no choice.

Kelsey couldn't stop herself from glancing down at Sergeant Jason Gould's hands as he made a show of inspecting his nails critically. They were cut short, uneven, and showed that he made his living with those hands—which made sense for a ramp gunner on an MH-47G Chinook. As one of the three crew chiefs, he'd have a dozen roles to serve—all of which said competent and strong. He was several inches taller than her own five-seven with an attractive leanness. She knew from his file that his family had a sportfishing business out of St. Petersburg, Florida. Curly dark hair and nearly black eyes.

She'd almost been attracted—if not for her hopelessness with attractive men. And the stupid hat.

"We'll go together, Jason. I need a mani-pedi anyway." Carmen. Dark red hair. Crew chief of the Chinook. Married to the co-pilot on the same craft. What a crazy outfit.

Five aboard the Chinook and four more aboard each of the two DAP Hawk gun platforms that would be flying protection. With her that made a total of fourteen flying tonight, plus two assets who had yet to arrive.

As Kelsey had no more control over the crew selection than the mission, she started the briefing. They might appear carefree, but the moment she began laying out the details of the mission, she had a hundred percent of their attention.

2

It was still mid-afternoon by the time the short briefing ended and they were into the hangar. The soft rain had turned downright wet.

Jason had been searching for an excuse to talk to Kelsey Killaney since the moment she'd hit the pavement at the 5E's compound. He found it when they stepped into the hangar.

"Stealth, ma'am. Every last bird." Their big Chinook, two DAP Hawks—Black Hawks turned into the world's most advanced gun platforms, and two Little Birds. The last wouldn't be on this mission, and the crews hadn't been called.

"I see that," she sounded a little breathless. "I've simply never heard of them."

"Must admit that we like it that way."

"It explains how," she looked at him puzzled for a moment, as if surprised to find herself talking to him. "How you do what you do."

"That, and the best crew flying." He still couldn't

believe that he was here. He supposed it was just being in the right place at the right time. After the Negev Desert disaster, they'd needed a new bird. The Army had provided them with the stealth configured *Calamity Jane II* and shipped them down to the 5E's team at Fort Rucker. Their mission pace had doubled and the complexity as well. He'd always simply been glad to be flying, but in the 5E he'd become more than he'd ever imagined.

And now, with Kelsey Killaney standing so close beside him that he could smell her fresh scent, like a strange winter flower, he started to understand just what he'd achieved. He was a goddamn flyer on the best bird in the sky, anywhere. Maybe, just maybe, he was good enough to stand next to a woman like her and not feel out of place.

They were following the rest of the crew up the rear ramp of the *Calamity Jane II*, prepping it for the first leg of the flight.

Her light brown hair was back in a severe ponytail that emphasized her large eyes. She was fair-skinned and had one of those smiles that looked as if it was always ready, even though she hadn't used it yet that he'd seen. The fact that she worked for The Activity said she was screamingly intelligent—an assumption borne out by the concise style of her briefing. If smart was the new sexy, she was a chart breaker—not that she wasn't by the old measure as well.

He'd truly done his best to pay attention at the briefing, but it had been hit and miss. He'd managed to sit next to her, by the simple stratagem of holding out a chair for her. But, no matter what he did, he couldn't get her to laugh. That hint of a smile hadn't even shifted when he'd started a whole riff about personal grooming tips off Carmen's mani-pedi remark—which was more Zoe the drone pilot's thing than Carmen's anyway.

Danny and the Captain were already in their seats running through checklists. Carmen and George were still outside pulling off pitot tube and air intake covers. So he had a moment and intended to use every second of it to his advantage.

"You need anything, ma'am? If so, I'm your man." He tried not to wince. Smooth as descending staircase on a tricycle—a trick he'd only tried once, but possibly where he got his taste for flying. He was getting no points for subtlety on this effort.

"Do you have a reality check somewhere?" Her question caused him to do a doubletake. So she did have a sense of humor behind her ever-so-serious facade.

"Somewhere, sure." Jason began patting the pockets of his flightsuit, peeked inside a couple of the pouches on his survival vest, and finally pulled a small pack of candy out of his medical supplies. "Will these do?"

Her expression turned into a dangerous scowl, "Hell no!"

He looked down to see if he'd mistakenly pulled out a grenade or a breaching charge, but he hadn't. "Who doesn't like Skittles?"

She sighed and rested a hand on his arm a moment as if apologizing.

Her fingers were almost delicate, but he could see a strength to them. She was so fit that he'd have guessed she was the sort who went to the high-end gym three times a week with a gaggle of girlfriends and had an impossibly handsome aerobics trainer named Julio

—*except* that she was Activity. The agents from The Activity were just as likely to go into the field to gather their own intel from behind enemy lines as they were to work at a desk in Fort Belvoir. They were known for being ruthlessly competent. Another thing he liked in a woman. If competence was the new sexy, then—

"Thanks for the offer and, yes, I do like Skittles. I just have this thing about Christmas, so thanks but no thanks."

He looked down at the little pack. It was clearly labeled Holiday Mix and showed only red and green flavors rather than the normal rainbow.

"Seems like you're putting a lot of weight on a little bit of seasonal packaging."

She nodded, "No argument from me. It's the one topic I'm a complete lunatic on."

"Christmas?"

"Christmas," she confirmed as if it was an incursion by an entire battalion of Taliban.

"Completely rational about everything else?"

"Everything!" Kelsey's tone was dry enough for him to laugh, which had several of the crew turning to look at him.

He squinted at Carmen, who had just come aboard and was checking over the internal systems, and mouthed, "What?"

Carmen shook her head, keeping her thoughts to herself, as she continued the pre-flight check.

*Fine!*

He tried to turn to give Carmen the cold shoulder, but she gave him an I-caught-you wink that blew his timing, even if he didn't know what she was on about.

"Even rational about men?" Jason turned back to

Kelsey.

"Always," then she grimaced, "for what good it has ever done me."

"I'm not sure if I should ask if that's a good sign or a bad one for me."

"As long as you're wearing that hat? Bad sign."

He looked up enough to spot the white, furry trim just above his eyebrows and remembered the blinking Rudolph.

"Nope," he looked back down at her and made a point of shaking his head hard enough to make the little bell at the end tinkle brightly. "Even being a gorgeous Activity agent, I'm not giving up my hat for you."

"Your loss," and finally that smile of hers came out. She did a quick turn and hair toss worthy of any disdainful supermodel, then strode up the cargo bay. But it was the smile that slayed him. From pretty to radiant faster than a heat-seeking missile.

He could only wonder what it would take to make her smile like that again. Taking off his hat? No. She'd smiled while making a joke because he had it on. He'd stick with a winning hand, no matter what she said about Christmas.

There had to be a reason behind it, but he wasn't sure how comfortable he felt digging for it with a complete stranger, no matter how attractive. It wasn't just her beauty. Something in her drew him—deeply. Not a feeling he was used to.

Done with the exterior inspection, George boarded as well and began checking his Minigun just as Carmen began going over hers. His own M240 hung out of the way in its bracket close by the rear ramp.

Kelsey sat in the observer's chair just behind the

pilots' seats. That should be safe, they were both married: the Captain to the unit's hot Italian drone pilot and quiet Danny—impossibly—to the vivacious Carmen. The only other crew member was the portside gunner and George was too British to try poaching where Jason had showed interest.

Out of excuses, Jason started his own preflight checks of the *Calamity Jane II* for a mission. Ammo full-stocked after the last mission was still fully stocked. Emergency supplies of food, water, and first aid were fully stocked and inside the refresh date. Enough to feed the whole crew for a week if they went down hard somewhere.

Then he started in puzzling on Kelsey. She must have her own reasons for being so *Bah Humbug!* But it didn't fit her. She seemed…happier than that.

Quiet. Which among the screaming extroverts of the 5E must be a shock. But there was something more. As if—

A high whine of fast-moving tires was all the warning he had to dodge out of the way before a pair of Polaris MRZRs came racing up the rear ramp. He jumped aside, clinging to the inside of the Chinook's hull to stay clear. The MRZRs were four-seater ATVs on Special Operations steroids. Tough, lightweight, fast, electric-quiet, and able to carry a thousand pounds of soldier and gear at sixty miles an hour or scramble over rough terrain at twenty. Except instead of the usual Army tan, they'd been painted like blue and red hotrods. Blinking Christmas lights had been wound around the bars of the roll cage which didn't make much sense unless…undercover as civilian hotrod dune buggies.

Right. Low profile mission. But had the woman who

hated Christmas thought of the Christmas lights? Jason suspected that she was the sort of woman who thought of everything and left nothing to chance.

The way the MRZRs raced aboard told him it was either SEAL or Delta at the helms.

Once they were in, he dropped back down. Both drivers wore clip-on fuzzy antlers.

"Duane? Dude! Haven't seen your ugly face since you left the Rangers for that wimp-ass Delta outfit." They'd stayed in close touch, but in four years had never managed to be in the same place at the same time.

"Jason, you Night Stalker piece of shit!" They thumped each other's backs hard enough to hurt.

"Cool antlers. Too bad they aren't half as cool as my hat." Then he spotted the gorgeous Latina stepping out of the other rig. She looked *very* cute in her antlers.

"You must be Sofia. I can't believe that you fell for a lump of coal like this one."

"He is all mine," she said in a happy, lushly Spanish accent, as she gave him a hug. "I have heard so many good things about you. I would know you anywhere by your so very silly hat."

"And if it hadn't been Christmas?"

"By your *very* good looks," she didn't hesitate to laugh.

Then she turned to Duane but kept an arm around Jason's waist so he kept his around her shoulders.

"I do not know," Sofia said thoughtfully. "Jason is *so* handsome. Why didn't you ever tell me this. Maybe I should be with a Night Stalker man and not a Delta boy."

With all the speed Jason would expect of a Delta operator, Duane hip-checked him into the emergency fire extinguishing system and separated Sofia with a quick hand about her waist—a move so smooth that it had all three of them laughing.

3

elsey sat at the far end of the helicopter's shadowed cargo bay and tried to look away. What would she give to be a part of that laughing circle of three? They looked so easy together, so effortlessly happy. That was a part of working for The Activity—she and the other analysts were a collection of loners, brought together by a fascination for the intricacies of information and an ability to turn it into actionable intelligence.

The folder that Colonel Gibson had provided was a perfect example. The first page had contained just three lines of information that suddenly brought her last six months of work into sharp focus.

*Delta Team and 160th SOAR 5E, Ech Stagefield, Fort Rucker*
*Juan Zavala, Christmas Eve*
(and an address in Cozumel)

It was Christmas Eve Day and Colonel Gibson had given her the first actionable lead on the elusive Juan Zavala that she'd seen in six months of hunting for him.

Zavala was one of the kingpins of the ultra-violent Jalisco New Generation cartel that she'd been tracing. The Jalisco were the former armed wing of the Sinaloa cartel and were rapidly gaining precedence in the Mexican drug scene. Under the kingpin theory of "take out the top and the internecine battles will do the rest of the cleanup," Zavala was a prime target.

She even recognized the address. It was a beach house that she had researched as one of his likely safe houses, but had never been able to trace him to.

Then the woman separated herself from the two men as they turned to arranging the two MRZRs more carefully and tying them down for flight. She moved through shadows until she was almost at Kelsey's side.

"Sofia?" She'd never expected to see Sofia Forteza again since she had left The Activity.

"Kelsey!" And Sofia gave her a hug as well which surprised her completely. Sofia had been one of her few friends at The Activity before she'd made the unlikely shift to Delta Force. But they'd never had a hugging kind of friendship.

"You seem happy."

"Ecstatic! I didn't know how much I loved being out in the field. Actually, I did know that. I know it better now. And Duane certainly helps," she was practically glowing as she aimed a happy look back down the bay.

"How do you know Jason?" Kelsey wasn't sure why she was asking. She'd watched them hug and felt... She didn't know. As if she wished it was her instead?

"I don't. It is the way that Duane talked about him, I

seem to already know him. They served in the US Rangers together. They've stayed very close."

Another skill Kelsey didn't have. She'd lost touch with Sofia the moment she'd headed over the horizon.

"Is this mission yours?" Sofia's effortless manners didn't give Kelsey enough time to feel uncomfortable.

She nodded.

"Good," Sofia nodded her head emphatically in return as the APU screamed to life and then the twin turbines began spinning up. "Then I know everything will go fine."

"You do?" Kelsey must have heard wrong over the building noise. A backwash of hot exhaust rippled through the cabin—it would clear as soon as they were moving. She'd been worrying about the mission every second since Colonel Gibson had handed her the file then evaporated or dropped through a trap door or whatever he'd done.

Sofia dug into her pocket and pulled out a pair of earplugs as the engine noise escalated. She shouted as she slid them in. "You were always the best planner we had when the terribles hit the fan. Except for me, of course. We all knew it and it made you a little scary to work with."

"I was?"

Past words, Sofia simply nodded before heading back down to rejoin the men.

People were scared of her?

Actually, that explained some reactions she'd observed. Rooms did seem to go quiet when she stepped into them, as if she was checking up on everybody. Except the 5E's briefing room. They were so skilled that maybe nothing daunted them.

What would it be like to work with them more? On occasion, an agent was permanently embedded with an elite team to facilitate operational communications more tightly with The Activity's specialties regarding human and signal intelligence. To be embedded with the 5th Battalion E Company would be both a challenge and… fun. Fun? That wasn't something she was very good at and erased the thought from her mind.

But she couldn't help glancing back down the cargo bay. Jason in his blinking Rudolph hat hadn't been afraid of her—just the opposite. He'd continued talking to her even after she'd snapped at him for offering her Christmas candy. Killjoy strikes again.

4

———

*K*elsey Killaney's plan sounded simple on the surface. Jason now knew that the surface appearances had nothing to do with one of Kelsey's plans.

She'd only outlined the basic approach strategy back at Fort Rucker: length of flights, refueling stops, necessary equipment. Per her instructions, beneath his flightsuit he wore slacks, a dress-shirt, and running shoes, though she hadn't explained why at the time. Under his shirt he wore a vest of lightweight Dragonskin armor for a bit of invisible protection.

She'd laid it out on the four-hour flight down to Naval Air Station Key West and refined it on the three-hour crossing to Cozumel after they'd eaten a hurried dinner while refueling. He'd never been to the small resort island off the Yucatan coast. Bringing a hot babe down here for a winter vacation had definitely been on his bucket list.

He'd never imagined that when he did it, he'd be unloaded after nightfall onto an empty stretch of beach ten miles across the island from the city of San Miguel de Cozumel. The weather was perfect. They'd left the storm somewhere over the Florida Keys and now drove out beneath a canopy of stars. Shirt sleeves were just right for the warm evening, though he could have done without the extra layer of the Dragonskin.

Night Stalkers usually didn't deploy on the active part of the mission, that's what Ranger door kickers and Delta operators were for. His job was to get them there, then shuffle away and hide until it was time to come fetch them.

Not on a Kelsey Killaney mission.

"I need an expert in flight operations on the mission team in case something goes wrong."

He'd considered arguing, until she said she was going as well.

"There isn't time to sufficiently brief everyone on the layout. We only have tonight, so I have to be there. I've spent too long hunting Zavala to let him slip away."

Which explained why she'd only requested two Delta operators rather than a full team.

"Can you drive?" Kelsey had asked as they were releasing the tie-downs on the vehicles.

"Sure." Of course he could.

"I mean really drive?"

"Dad ran sprint car races for a hobby. If he paid the entry fee, then got a sportfishing client, I'd drive the race for him. I was a much better driver than I was a fisherman." Then he climbed into the driver's seat of the MRZR and buckled in to settle the point. An MRZR was a close relative of a sprint car. Four seats instead of one, no airfoil on the top, and an MRZR had an engine that could only go sixty, not a hundred and sixty. But those were the differences. In common, they both had: an open metal frame with a serious roll cage, a very low center of gravity, demon-like cornering abilities, and were made for running in the sand and dirt and being fast while doing it.

In the far back, an MRZR had an extra space like a miniature pickup. It could carry two extra soldiers or a pile of gear. Right now, they had massive tourist drink coolers—coolers that were loaded with all of their tactical gear and most of the weapons they had just illegally smuggled into a friendly country. Due to corruption, the results on these types of missions were often better if the foreign government wasn't notified. The challenge was to not be caught in the process as that tended to upset them badly.

It was only as they rolled off the back of the Chinook and onto the deserted beach, that the truth clicked in.

"You already knew that I could really drive. That's why you didn't get a second driver for this mission from Delta."

"Maybe I just like your hat," Kelsey said it as if she was all innocence. No, she said it like a tease—like maybe the first tease she'd ever made.

He drove up the beach and over the berm onto the Quintana Roo road, then waited for Duane and Sofia to join them in the second MRZR. How had that lucky bastard gotten a woman like that? Sofia was beyond beautiful, right up there in Kelsey Killaney's category. And she was a Delta Force fighter. As far as he knew, they had like three women in the entire unit, yet somehow Duane had won her heart. And not just a little. Married if that didn't beat all. The only man less likely to get married in their Ranger platoon than one Jason Gould.

That got Jason thinking about why he himself was that way. Because he was stupid? Or because he'd never met the right woman? He'd take answer B any day. Any day before now. He wasn't sure why she fascinated him so much, but that was a question he was willing to pursue.

"You hate my hat," he reminded her.

"You're right. I hate your hat."

"And how important is it that we go low profile undercover here?"

"Why do you think we repainted the MRZRs in hotrod colors and are wearing civilian clothes?"

"But you hate my hat."

She glared over at him.

"That's too bad." He wasn't quite sure why he'd grabbed the extra accessory when getting civilian clothes out of his room, but he had.

"Why? Because you so *love* your hat?"

"I do, but that's not the problem," he tried to shake his head as if she was pitiful.

Duane and Sofia cleared the berm and pulled up beside them on the empty highway as the helos disappeared back into the night: the big Chinook and the two guardian DAP Hawks. They'd fly out well beyond radar range and refuel from a circling C-130 tanker while they waited.

"Then what's the problem, Jason?" Kelsey's guard was down just enough that if he was quick…

He pulled out his second hat, triggered the flashing nose, and pulled it onto her head. Her hair was impossibly sleek, so smooth it might have been ice, but was so warm and human that it seemed to burn his hand. He yanked his hands away before he could do more.

"There," he declared. Stomping on the gas, he unleashed the MRZR. It leapt down the road with Duane and Sofia close behind. "Now you're low profile."

"I'm going to have to kill you, Jason," she shouted over the racing wind.

"Wait until after the mission, okay?"

5

Kelsey tugged the hat down against the speed-generated wind and hated herself for it. Hated that she hated Christmas. Hated that she still didn't know how to be nice to Jason when he'd been nothing but nice to her. Wearing his stupid matching hat was the first concession she'd managed.

He looked over and grinned at her as he turned left onto the Carretera Transversal to cross the island.

"So, tell me why you're irrational about Christmas?" He shouted over the wind noise. The electric MRZR itself was quiet, but there was roaring wind and the tire noise as they raced the 9.3 miles across the island in a vehicle with no windshield. The wide two-lane road ran straight as an arrow between two uninterrupted walls of green—their headlights well-focused on the road ahead so that they'd be hard to spot from any distance.

Not a chance. "Tell me why you're so crazy for it that you have not one but two Rudolph hats."

They covered a mile in silence before he spoke. He slowed a little, but the road noise barely changed.

"Mom bought them for Dad and I last Christmas. This one is his," he tapped his forehead. "You're wearing mine."

"Why do you have *his* hat? Thief!" She was suddenly very conscious of having Jason's hat on her head. It was so…personal. As if they were together—somehow a couple.

Again the mile-long pause.

"The cancer killed Dad by Valentine's Day. Mom followed him, of a broken heart by July Fourth."

Kelsey felt as if she'd just been punched. She reached out and clamped a hand over his arm in sympathy. Could feel his muscles rippling beneath the surface as he drove. His strength a comfort, when she should be the one providing that.

"Sorry," he steadfastedly stared ahead without a glance toward her. "It just slips out sometimes. When I'm not being careful."

Kelsey could only look at him in amazement. His ridiculous hat and teasing her about it had more meaning than should be possible. In an instant he transformed from a ridiculous man who had been kind to her, to a kind man who didn't mind being perceived as ridiculous—even if he wasn't.

How was he so comfortable in his own skin that he could do that?

She was on the verge of asking, but knew that wasn't right. He'd just laid his heart out on the cross-Cozumel road. His honesty demanded the same.

"My parents hated each other. I still don't know why they stayed together."

Kelsey's hand still rode lightly on Jason's forearm,

but she was reluctant to take it away. Through it, she could feel a listening stillness come over him.

"But they didn't fight all year. Instead, they saved all of their bitterness for one 'special season'," she wished she could do this softly rather than shouting it in short choppy sentences with no ability to gauge her listener's reaction. "The Christmas tree. Mom thinks they're pretty. Dad hates them as a waste of money, space, time… I don't know. It's not like we were poor. Maybe he hates them because Mom likes them. Dad would pick the fight starting in October. Stretch it into February when he was on a roll."

Jason's stillness continued as the lights of San Miguel de Cozumel city began to light the road ahead of them.

"Christmas is nothing but bad memories."

Jason slowed as they entered the outskirts of the city. He hadn't said a word as she'd told him something that she'd never told anyone. She'd always managed to keep her *Bah Humbug!* to herself before. Somehow was never dating anyone when Christmas came around, always opting out of Secret Santa at work. She'd stressed herself into actual illness before any number of Christmas parties.

And Jason just drove.

"Look."

She was looking, to see what his reaction to her was. For some reason it seemed to matter, but she couldn't read it.

Then he nodded to either side of the road.

She looked. There were breaks in the trees. Houses that were little more than hovels were tucked in among palm and avocado trees. And each one had bright Christmas lights. Sometimes just a doorway, sometimes a spiral climbing a palm tree, and frequently a lit creche of the birth in the manger in gaudy plastic. The closer they got to town, the more extravagant the displays.

They turned southwest on the Avenida Rafael E. Melgar.

The waterfront was a wonder of lights. To her right lay the sea. Cruise ship docks jutted out into the dark ocean—the ships lit like cities of their own. Hundreds and hundreds of people strolled along the seawall. Most holding hands or in close groups chattering happily together.

The street was divided by a narrow median with a palm tree every hundred feet or so, and each was brightly wound in Christmas lights. The one- and two-story whitewashed shops along the inland side of the street were a bounty of Christmas displays.

Jason continued to drive in silence.

People waved at them in their two colorfully lit MRZRs, dressed up so that they looked like high-end dune buggies. She waved back.

They passed a tall lighthouse close by the cruise terminal. It cast no light. Yet even from here, in the brightest heart of the promenade, she could see the tall beacon to the south that had replaced it—two white flashes every five seconds.

Was that herself? A decommissioned lighthouse amidst an abundance of light?

She turned back to Jason as he continued easing along in the southbound traffic. Was he the beacon that now flashed so brightly ahead? Somehow he was holding onto the joy that his dead parents had taught him while she was still wrapped up in the darkness that her parents had tried to teach her.

It was a crappy metaphor, especially if it was true and she was the decommissioned lighthouse.

Up ahead there was another light, far taller and flashing brightly. That looked like a much happier metaphor, if she could figure out how to live it.

6

"*I* don't want to feel decommissioned any more." Kelsey slipped her hand off his arm and he missed it. He missed the comfort. He missed the connection.

"What?" Jason wondered where that had come from. He was still trying to shake off the memories of last Christmas, his dad already past being able to speak, but smiling as he wore his goofy hat. Meager presents opened on a hospital bed because no one could find the energy to shop for more.

"The lighthouses," Kelsey pointed upward.

Jason hadn't even noticed them. He could barely see anything other than the withered man who took up so little space on the vast bed.

"You think you're a decommissioned lighthouse?"

"Can't prove otherwise by me."

He'd heard her story, about her idiot parents. Had they somehow pounded into this beautiful woman's head that she wasn't worth better?

Jason had asked Sofia about her, when it was clear they knew each other.

"Not much to tell. Brilliant, driven, the very best in very tough crowd. But she really keeps herself to herself, if you understand what I am meaning. She never talks about anything outside of the missions. So it's not as if I'm giving anything away because neither will she."

But Kelsey just had. To him.

"Kelsey?"

"Uh-huh."

"How could you get something so completely wrong?"

"What? I know where Zavala is. I know the layout of the house. We are the perfect assets to do this fast and quiet." She was back on the mission, and she was right. They'd rolled past the flashing lighthouse, leaving behind traffic, another cruise terminal, and once more were into the outskirts of the rapidly disappearing town.

"There," she pointed. They dropped down onto the narrow shore road past the big resorts, the Chankanaab Beach Resort being the last of them. He had a quick glimpse of a quiet lagoon and thatched huts. It was the sort of place he'd imagined bringing a woman, though not with a load of weapons, rather with a bikini and a lot of time with nothing planned.

They continued south along the shore. The low beach and berm were usually close by, except when lush estates pushed the access road inland.

"Here," Kelsey pointed again.

He turned off into a vacant lot. It made a gap through the scrub trees and palms connecting the road to the beach. He stopped before they reached the sand. The electric MRZRs were silent and he could hear the gentle splash of the waves picked out in the headlights. He and Kelsey here, together. It was very easy to imagine.

Duane and Sofia rolled up quietly behind them, but Jason ignored them.

Instead, he turned to Kelsey. Her face was randomly lit by the blinking Christmas lights on the roll cage. The shifting shadows made it hard to read her expression.

"It's Christmas Eve," he said, for lack of any better ideas.

"It is," she looked down at her folded hands.

"Got a present for you."

"Better than this hat?" Then he saw her bite her lower lip because she now obviously understood the importance of the hat. He'd only been teasing when he put it on her, but it had gained so much meaning in the last half hour.

"Well, okay, it's not *that* cool, but I'm making this up as I go."

She only nodded, but it was quick, accepting. Then she appeared to brace herself.

He dug in his pocket and pulled out the bag of Christmas Skittles, handing it across solemnly.

Kelsey stared down at it for a long time before taking it gently from his hands.

"To hell with your past," he told her. "To hell with mine. New beginnings. Though I figured I was safer to start small." It was also the only thing he had to give at the moment.

She looked up at him with her dark eyes so wide that they seemed to catch all of the colors of the Christmas lights at once.

Then she clutched the little packet of candy to her

chest with both hands, and nodded for him to continue down the beach.

The plan was fiendishly simple—he wondered if all of Kelsey's plans were like that. If so, she absolutely belonged in the 5E. It was beyond stealth…it was cool! And so much better than the home invasion that was their backup scenario.

They drove the two Christmas-decorated MRZRs slowly down the beach. In front of each beach house before Zavala's, they stopped and sang Christmas carols. When her clear soprano joined in, it really brought it to life. The owners came out, offered punch and apple fritters at one house and orange sugar cookies at the next. Each stop drew out the owners of the next residence along the beach front.

At Zavala's, the last in the row, the pattern held. Zavala came out to hear them and brought a bottle of rum. On the last stretch of darkened beach, they knocked out his two guards with dart guns they'd stashed under the seats, drugged Zavala and his equally dangerous brother as well before tying them in back of the MRZRs, and continued on their way as if nothing had happened. His capture only took seconds.

Just inland was the little-used Aeródromo Capitán Eduardo Toledo. A small field used for tourist flights during the day, and nothing at night. The Chinook slipped in and they drove up the cargo bay ramp so fast that the helo barely stopped.

Once they were aloft and clear of Cozumel, Kelsey came to find him where he was leaning against the angle of the raised rear ramp—his normal post as tail gunner.

She still wore the hat.

And she opened her joined hands for just a moment

to show that she still clutched the little packet of candy, before once more holding it to her chest. And her eyes, those wide, lovely eyes looked ready to take on the world.

Then she leaned in to kiss him. Not some quick thank you peck, but soft, lush, so full of warmth that for a moment he felt as if he was indeed lying on a sunny Cozumel beach with her.

"Thank you," she whispered from mere inches away.

Jason tried to come up with some quip. Something to ease the moment for the lady in the blinking Rudolph hat. But all he could think to whisper back was the same, "Thank *you.*"

He'd assumed this Christmas would be hell, because of the memories of the last one. Instead, she'd given him the gift of hope as a present.

When she kissed him again, this time letting herself curl up against him, he had hope for the many Christmases to come as well.

# SERGEANT GEORGE AND
# THE DRAGOON

**Royal Air Force Colour Sergeant George Hayman's** *year flying with the Night Stalkers 5E ends in three days. His final mission starts well—but then goes terribly wrong. He finally feels he has some grip on American idiom, but being shot was "no picnic."*

*The biggest shock? Nothing in his training prepared him for the nameless but lovely French dragoon who falls into his lap —literally.*

*Their missions flying with the Americans are over, but that only begins the tale of Sergeant George and the Dragoon.*

# INTRODUCTION

*C*uriously, this story too was born from a Delta Force novel just as *Since the First Day* had been.

I was starting my final Delta novel, *Midnight Trust,* in which total mayhem is going on. The hero climbs aboard a Chinook helicopter, yes, the *same* Chinook helicopter, as part of a two-team extraction.

The second team's extraction turns into a rescue from a major gun battle. The heroine boards the helo, briefly, before she and the hero are dumped out—over a waterfall—to start their own adventure.

However, a couple of curious things happened during that opening battle scene.

One person aboard had a British accent.

And I was having trouble with accounting for the number of survivors from the second team.

By now I knew what that meant…a new short story!

Special Operations Forces are incredibly unique in several ways that took me, as a non-military-type person, some time to figure out.

There are regular forces.

Special Forces, at least in the US, means the Green Berets. While they're tough as can be fighters, they also have a crossover role of community relations. You'll find them having meetings with leaders or building schools— in addition to leaping into the heat of battle.

Special *Operations* Forces are trained almost exclusively for one task—fighting. Now it could be a quiet "black" operation, a hostage rescue, or a surgical strike, but these folks are fighters first, second, and third.

The 75th Rangers, SEALs, Delta Force, SEAL Team 6, the UK and Australian SAS, the French Dragoons, the Russian Spetsnaz, and so on. These are the SOF, the elite.

One of the things that these elite units do, at least the ones friendly with each other, is officer exchange programs. Charlie Beckwith spent a year on exchange with the UK's Special Air Service, and returned to the US with the self-assigned mission to create Delta Force.

So, I knew that my subconscious had included that British accent for a reason—my hero was an exchange officer from the UK.

I also knew from the book's opening that he'd been injured.

This took me back to my some of my early writing habits. The characters in the 5D were rarely injured. If they were hit, they were typically killed outright, with the notable exceptions of Archie Stevenson's shoulder and Emily Beale's…ahem, behind.

There are far more injuries than deaths among actual fighting forces and I hadn't done much with that outside of my Henderson's Ranch stories.

It was time to start exploring those who survived, but who should counterpoint my wounded hero?

He's English.

Who were the English at war with for centuries?

The French.

And I had my injured heroine.

1

———————————

One year minus three days.

Colour Sergeant George Hayman was counting the days, but not for the reasons he had expected. When his commander had told him that he was to be a foreign-military exchange liaison with the Americans of the 160th Night Stalkers 5th Battalion E Company, his protests fell on deaf ears.

"They're the most advanced helicopter company the Yanks have flying, sergeant. Besides, you are one of the very few who has the security clearance they require."

*Because of your family connections,* he didn't say.

George's father was an unspecified, but *very* highly placed official in MI-6, the foreign intelligence service. It had made Father's life easier for George and Mother to be cleared to SC status or better. It had let Father sit in the parlor with them while reading through his less classified files. George's own work with the Special Forces 7th Squadron RAF had led him to get the DV— Developed Vetting—the UK's highest-level clearance as well.

To this day, Father never spoke about anything he was working on. Or even precisely who he worked for. It remained rather unclear whether that was due to information compartmentalization or to Father being a taciturn bastard—George felt he was finally getting a good 'handle' on American euphemism after a year minus three days. He favored the latter conclusion.

Either way, his DV clearance meant that he had what the Yanks were after. And his commander had chosen him for the assignment.

"But, sir, they are always so…full of themselves."

"Bottle it, I believe the Americans say."

"I think it's 'Jar it,' sir." (He knew better now.)

"Jar it, then. Cowboys or not, I need to learn what they know. So, gather your hounds and drain your stirrup cup, or whatever you types do."

"Saddle up, sir." He was going to America, after all.

And one-year-minus-three-days ago, he'd landed in the sweltering wilderness of Fort Rucker, Alabama. Such places were fit for neither man nor beast, but they *were* fit for perhaps the finest crew he'd ever served with. He was going to be sorry to go back home. The weather had turned out to not be an issue because the 5E's mission tempo was so high that they were rarely *at* Fort Rucker. Instead they were in places sufficiently awful to make Mother Rucker (as the fort was known) appear actually palatable.

Even stranger, the lead pilot on the *Calamity Jane II*— a huge MH-47G Chinook helicopter—was indeed a cowboy, a real one. Captain Justin Roberts came from a long line of Texas horse breeders and wore his Stetson whenever he wasn't wearing his flight helmet. The others on the crew had come from wildly varied backgrounds—each incredibly impressive in his own way. Or *her* own way.

He'd landed as their starboard-side gunner and second crew chief to Sergeant Carmen Parker. A talkative, funny, and outspoken redhead who knew more about how and why helicopters worked than anyone he'd ever met. Working with her hadn't been a honing of his craft; it had been a Level 8 doctoral program in its own right in both operations and strategy.

And now there were only three days left before his return to the UK.

"Last mission," he meant it for himself, but he still wasn't used to the always-live intercom that this team favored.

"I don't know, gang," Carmen called out. "We gonna miss him?"

He'd finally learned to not be hurt by Carmen's teases, but it had taken a long time to understand that she only teased people she liked—and to them she was merciless.

A chorus of "Nah!" "Nope!" and "Not a chance!" sounded over the headphones in his helmet.

"Right back to you, you undeserving lot." They were the most deserving team he'd ever met. A Brit nuanced their feelings. The Americans were possessed of no nuance at all. Their use of a single emphatic word, where five would do nicely, made it terribly difficult to isolate sarcasm from forthright intent.

Carmen sounded a loud raspberry, telling him that he'd managed to get the hang of it well enough before he left—if not by much.

"Try not to screw us up on your last flight, mate,"

Carmen called out as they swung down for the second extraction of the night.

'Mate' was Strine from Down Under, not British. He had attempted to correct that on his second day—and his third and fourth. It turned out to be something Carmen had apparently already known and all of his protests had only served to embed it deeply in her repertoire.

Their first recovery tonight had happened quietly— a single Delta Force recon specialist had strolled out of the Colombian jungle at twilight and stepped onto the helicopter's lowered rear ramp before it even touched the ground. He'd worn full jungle camo and enough gear on his massive frame to intimidate anyone. *Solo* recon. The Delta operators were even crazier than the SAS he normally carried around back home.

The second extraction was occurring at a cliff edge over a fast-running river after night had fallen. The jungle itself was a hundred meters back, but there was no clear spot to set down atop the cliff edge. So, they were forced to hover *beyond* the cliff edge. As the helo swung into position—tail ramp touching the stone and the long body of the helo hovering a hundred feet above the river—the jungle roared to life.

Not just monkeys and parrots and whatever other denizens resided there. Rather, the trees were suddenly alive with more muzzle flashes than he could count. He hit the power switch on his M134D minigun, grabbed onto the twin handles—

And was thrown down to the steel deck—*hard!*

For a second he didn't know what had hit him. The gun was driven by an electric motor, but the jolt hadn't come through his hands. Then he understood the problem. Despite the helo's armor at his position, and the large weapon sitting in the middle of the small window, a stray round had found a gap and drilled into his arm.

OMG but he understood the problem!

His upper arm had been punched by no teasing blow of Carmen knuckling the triceps nerve cluster.

This was a hammer of pain that no training instructor had ever handed out. The big Delta guy strolled up to him and squatted as if he was inspecting a mosquito bite.

"Huh," he wrapped a bandage around it which caused George to blank for a second as the pain slammed in double-fold. He came to as the Delta finished putting George's arm in a sling. He was leaning against the side of the hull now, out of everyone's way.

"Better have someone look at that when you get back to base."

"Ruddy hell yeah!" Did the guy think he was going to just walk around with it until some fairy godmother magically healed it? Or had that been more backward American understatement?

Then the guy stepped up to the minigun and took over firing it.

George shoved his visor out of his way. When he'd been hurled back, he must have become disconnected from the umbilical that projected data on the inside of his visor. With it out of the way, he now lay in the cargo bay, surreally awash with the dim red of night operations lighting.

Digging one-handed into his own medkit, George found a fentanyl lollipop. It looked more like a white multi-vitamin on a stick. Once he managed to get it out of its foil pack—never meant to be done one-handed with a hand shaking from the pain—and tucked into his cheek, the pain backed off.

*Way* off! No wonder there were all the training warnings about how addictive these things were. A shot of morphine both punched the pain and punched you under. This felt great. It almost convinced him that he could stand up and do a little fighting himself, though the Delta seemed to be doing a 'bang-up' job by the sound of it.

George slouched against the inside of the helo and listened to the buzz-saw roar of the minigun lashing out four thousand rounds per minute in two- and three-second bursts.

One. Two. Three.

The guy shifted angles.

One. Two.

He didn't quite have the waltz beat that George had found useful to hum while firing, but he was close enough. Short, sharp, focused firing was the trick.

One. Two. *Clank!*

*Clank?* That wasn't a good sound. He looked up to see the guy testing the barrel spin. That looked normal, but the ammunition belt wasn't moving.

"Sounds like you sheared the pin in the delinker. Two-dollar part, but takes ten minutes to replace it." He was pretty impressed that he could put those thoughts together. The fentanyl was definitely doing its job—he felt light, as if he might start floating.

"We've got, like, thirty seconds," the guy whinged.

George shrugged his indifference—then wished like hell he hadn't. The fentanyl was good, but the pain from the ill-considered movement slammed in hard and his vision tunneled badly.

For a time, there were just intermittent flashes of consciousness.

A military MRZR all-terrain vehicle with four soldiers aboard racing up the rear ramp.

Some shouting.

A body dumped across his lower legs.

The MRZR and the Delta gone.

More shouting.

None of it from the body lying on him.

No blood on their back.

Being careful of his arm, he rolled the soldier over so that now he was lying across George's thighs instead of his calves. He landed with a groan of life.

Definitely blood on the front, the trousers were soaked in blood—which showed up as black beneath the helo's red light. And the soldier was clearly awake and in intense pain—eyes squeezed shut hard and teeth gritted.

The female soldier.

Unable to face the challenge of his med kit again, he pulled the fentanyl lollipop out of his mouth and stuck it in hers.

He definitely missed it as he began basic triage even if logic said that it couldn't wear off that fast. It certainly felt as if it did.

Her leg was wrong. Very wrong.

"Medic!" he shouted, but no one appeared to be listening. Carmen was still manning the other minigun. Another was wielding a fire extinguisher at something. The last soldier was still looking out the rear ramp where the MRZR had disappeared into the night. The only other person in the cargo bay was lying against the far side of the hull—with his eyes open and his jaw slack. Bad sign. Very bad.

The woman in his lap fainted and her face relaxed. Not much to see beneath the camouflage battle paint. He checked, she still had a pulse. Apparently it was up to him to keep that going.

Him, the one-armed man.

One year minus three days.

Go figure! (He was fairly sure that he had that idiom right.)

2

arta Proulx came to with a tasteless lollipop in her mouth. She'd always been partial to *sucette—citron* was her favorite. She loved anything lemon. Her mother's lemon tarts were the best of any French pastry shop. This *sucette* had nothing to like about it, but she couldn't find the energy to spit it out.

A man was tugging at her clothes.

She hit him.

Or tried to.

She felt as weak as a kitten and barely managed to hit him at all.

He shrieked as if she'd run him down with a her Peugeot.

"Do not do that ever again," the man glared down at her. His accent was very British. Posh British.

"Then stop, *monsieur,* with the taking off of my clothes." Somewhere in there was a coherent sentence.

"I will if you agree to stop bleeding."

"I'm bleeding?" She shouldn't be bleeding. Then she

166

remembered the race through the jungle. Hostiles sprouting up faster than the foliage—which was definitely saying a lot. Most of her career had been in Southwest Asian deserts. The incredible bio-density of South American jungles still startled her every time, even though she'd been here for six months.

"Bleeding copiously," the Brit observed.

"Well…" she tried to connect the thought to something, but it was a hard struggle. "Make it stop."

"Hence, the removal of your clothes," he waved a pair of shears at her.

"Oh. Cut away."

The gun battle that she could only vaguely recall faded away. The few crew members in the cargo bay were rushing about as if their was a great cause for alarm, but Marta was having trouble concentrating enough to see what it was.

To block them out, she closed her eyes and tried to imagine that it was a cool spring day back home in Chartres. Sitting out on the cobbled square with a treat from *La Chocolaterie* on the Place du Cygne. The sun warm, the tourists to the Chartres gothic cathedral not yet thick as flies…

Each tug on her trousers destroyed the image with fresh jolts of pain.

"Be careful, you cocky swine." She'd served with enough Brits to know what they all were.

"You French are always whinging. I'm doing the best I can one-handed."

"Then use two hands, fool." That's when she noticed he had one arm in a sling and was sweating badly. More than might be called for by the jungle's heat. Actually, he shouldn't be sweating at all; there was a pleasant draft flowing through the helicopter.

The helicopter?

Unsure of how she came to be here, she looked around.

"Where's the rest of the crew?" It seemed there should be more people here. No sign of Tanya, her team leader. Somehow she'd driven through hell to get them here, but where was she now?

The Brit waved his shears across the helo. Barely visible beneath the red nightlights she stared into Carl's blank face. He lay crumpled against the other side of the hull and didn't look as if he'd be moving again except into a body bag. She closed her eyes, not wanting to see more.

"It's not going well, is it?" She asked but kept her eyes tightly closed.

"I don't know. The wound looks clean, just bloody. Can you raise your knee?" With his assistance, she managed to, and thanks to the fentanyl, managed to do it without shrieking like a schoolgirl. Even as a schoolgirl she'd never been the sort to shriek.

"Marta has displayed a fine attention to her studies. However, she is not a team player—she strives to be the best, which is not very humble. Worse, she does so, uncaring of the cost to everyone around her." Sister Mary Patrick had sounded almost gleeful in reporting the fault to her mother.

Sister Mary Patrick was wrong. Marta was a fine team player, once she found a team worth playing for like—

"Ahh!"

"What?"

"My leg, it is not supposed to have a hole in it." She should have kept her eyes closed. By propping her knee up, he'd been able to cut away the rest of the material around her thigh. And now she could see where the round had sliced through. It wasn't arterial bleeding or she'd be dead, but it was very bloody.

"At least yours was a meat shot. I think I lost a section of bone." He spread a small line of superglue on the bullet hole, then squeezed the edges together. He groaned as he twisted around to glue what must be the exit hole on the back of her thigh.

She tried to close her eyes, but couldn't help watching. Despite his injuries, he was gentle.

"Bloody hell!"

"What?"

"Nothing," he said too quickly.

"*What?*" Was the sudden chill of the breeze over the steel deck just imagined, or was it from soon-to-be-terminal blood loss and shock?

"I just glued my sling to your thigh."

He began to remove the sling and she could see the agony across his features. Even if he was a Brit, no one deserved that.

She held out the fentanyl lollipop and tucked it into his mouth the next time he groaned.

He finally managed to extract his arm from the sling and sit upright once more.

He dug into her medkit which she wore over her stomach. It actually tickled a little despite her armored vest between them. He pulled out a triangular bandage and fashioned a second sling.

"You know..." She reached out to help him settle it in place.

"What?" His breath was still a hiss as they got his arm settled.

"You had a pair of shears."

"You're suggesting perhaps that I would have been better served had I snipped your leg off? In retrospect, I'm inclined to agree."

"No. But you might have snipped off the corner of the sling."

"Huh!" His grunt sounded very American. He pulled out the fentanyl lollipop and inspected it carefully.

After exchanging a woeful glance, he chucked it up into the airflow and it whipped out the rear ramp of the racing helo and into the night.

"Blast," he sighed as he cradled his arm and leaned back against the helo's vibrating hull.

The last thing Marta recalled was lying in the Brit's lap as exhaustion, fentanyl, and blood loss finally combined to take her under.

3

e opened his eyes.

White.

Lots and lots of white.

It started at George's shoulder. Blinking hard to bring it into focus, he managed to follow the line of it all of the way to his fingertips. Those stuck out the end of the fiberglass cast that dangled from a sling above him.

Would they wiggle?

Did he want to know if they didn't?

Taking a deep breath, he tried. They did. Everything from shoulder to wrist was a land of numb, but he could wiggle his fingers and feel the round edges of the cast. Victory!

Everything else was white as well. The ceiling, the walls, the sheets.

*Hospital* white.

Uh-oh.

So *not* a good sign. (*Nailed the idiom,* some thought reported through the fog that seemed to wrap around him. Or should it have been: *So* not a good sign? With an elongated 'o'? Whatever. *Oh god, another idiom. Shut up!*)

Then he refocused on the cast on his arm. Perhaps being in hospital made a modicum of sense.

The bed beside his was white as well, except for the woman lying atop the covers. She was the only color in the room—fantastically so. Long brunette hair that ruffled over her pillow (white) with chocolate brown eyes to match. Her face sported the lovely high cheekbones and full lips of the French.

"*Bon matin!*"

Ha! He had nuked it…nailed it. One of those things.

She *was* French.

"Good morning…I suppose." George blinked again and saw more white—this time her gauze-wrapped leg stretched across the sheet (more white). "Oh! It's you. The woman with the leg."

"Well, I was thinking hard about transforming into someone else—someone who hadn't been shot—but that hasn't been working very well for me. It's the first time anyone has recognized me by my legs."

"They're nice legs." He must still be drugged to utter such a remark. But they were. She looked splendidly long and lovely stretched out atop the covers in her hospital gown. He appreciated the lack of length in the gown's hem.

"They were nicer before they were shot twice."

"Twice?" He tried to jolt upright. The painkiller kept the pain at bay, but the cast extended up onto his shoulder and it weighted him into place.

"*Calme,*" she instructed in the wonderful accent of hers.

"Where else were you hit?" The horror that he might have left her to bleed to death because he hadn't checked for other wounds was overwhelming.

"Nowhere else. Once I was shot from in front and once I was shot from behind. Two separate damage paths, which is why there was so much blood. You… saved my life."

"My pleasure, ma'am. You don't exactly sound pleased."

"I don't enjoy being beholden to any man."

"Perhaps if I were a woman."

That earned him a light laugh that sounded even more French than her lovely accent. "It does not go well with your three-day growth of beard. Which looks good on you, by the way."

"My what?" He rubbed his chin, and it was definitely there. "Three days?"

"We both spent the day after the mission in surgery. We're in an Aruban hospital, by the way—the closest Western hospital to our extraction point. Yours was rather more drastic, they had to remove a section of bone and replace it with a titanium rod."

He did note that neither of them were on life monitors or IV drips which he supposed practically made them outpatients. A good sign.

"You slept through yesterday."

George could only stare at the ceiling in shock. This was now the third day since his injury, which meant that his year with the Night Stalkers was over. He was going to miss them horribly.

"I'm done."

"No you aren't!" Marta was startled by his defeatist tone. "The doctors expect a full recovery." The damage to her own leg was almost as severe. Her bones hadn't been broken, but the bullets had tumbled and ripped up tendon and muscle badly. But no one was going to stop her from getting back into the battle.

"No, I mean I'm done here."

"You're quitting? You qualified to fly on a Night Stalkers helicopter and you're quitting because you were shot. What did you think Special Operations was? A child's game? Stupid British fool. Yes, I called you a fool before and I was right to do so."

She could hear that she was unleashing *la tempête de Marta* as the nuns had called the storm of her temper, but it was something she'd never managed to truly control. Especially not when someone was being so foolish.

Yes, she had been a poor team player in Catholic school. That was only because she hadn't found a truly superior team until she'd joined the 13th Parachute Dragoons.

"Hey, uh… What's your name anyway?"

"I am not telling some British quitter." Never. Neither hot pincers nor bad pastries would—

"I'm not quitting, whoever you are." His tone was sharp. Especially sharp considering that he was British. That made it especially cutting—roughly the same level as the French sniff of disdain.

"But you just said— Foof!" She wiggled her fingers at him in dismissal and give him the disdainful sniff. "Now you are a liar."

"No. Now I am once again a member of the No. 7 Squadron in Her Majesty's Royal Air Force."

"I thought you were a Night Stalker."

"A one-year exchange. Which ends today. I'm done."

"Is that what you meant?"

He nodded solemnly.

"*Un moment.* The 7th Squadron?"

"Yes, I'm a helo crew chief for Chinook helicopters."

"No, you aren't. You fly for Joint Special Forces. They're the very best of the UK. And you just spent a year flying with the Night Stalkers?" Now that was a man who definitely would play at the same level she did.

He offered only a tight nod.

"I'm just finishing six months with an inter-force recon team. I'm with the 13th." And now she would see if he really was who he said he was, by how he responded. If he gave her the standard "You're kidding, right?", she was going to punch his arm again—much harder now that she wasn't dying from blood loss.

His low whistle of surprise said he knew what it was.

"The 13th *Régiment de Dragons Parachutistes*." He even managed the pronunciation reasonably well and knew that dragoon in French was *dragon*.

She had fought so hard to make it into the dragoon regiment of France's Spec Ops. No one understood how hard it was. Not the Catholic sisters, not her mother, not any of the regular military she met. Not even the men who had applied and failed. They would brag to her about their failed attempts as if it was the high point of their lives—as if she would ever accept a lover who had failed.

"No wonder you want to be beholden to no man— or woman with a three-day beard."

Curiously, she believed that *he* understood how hard she'd fought to reach her goal.

5

George faded out before he learned her name.

He faded back in for doctors and once more for food, both of which she slept through. They, or their drugs, were badly out of sync.

Which was too bad. Because now it was two in the morning and he was wide awake with only the soft rattle of the air conditioning to keep him company.

He had learned so much over the last year to take back to his home unit. Carmen had taught him shortcuts that weren't shortcuts, they were just ten times more efficient than how the manual said to perform a task. Captain Roberts and Danny Corvo, his copilot, had obliged him with well-considered answers to his endless questions. Their innovations in overlapping minigun coverage and infiltration techniques were going to shake up some of the 'good old boys' back home.

And the lovely woman from the 13th dragoons of France had captivated his thoughts. Special Operations women were a rare commodity in any country's military. It wasn't for lack of need; rather, in his opinion, most women lacked a certain bloody-mindedness. Carmen had been a prime example of what he'd always thought was needed for a woman to succeed in Spec Ops—her attitude was as rough-and-tough as any male's, maybe more than most. Yet, no matter how she might act, Carmen was also the core of the team as much or more than its captain. Women brought a cohesiveness that a mere 'band of brothers' often lacked.

The woman lying beside him had that steel core—and a matching spark of temper. But she was so very purely female. Perhaps it was because she was French—

The woman lying *beside* him?

"How did we end up in the same room?" He asked the darkness.

"I have been wondering that myself," the darkness answered.

"You're awake?" He could feel the weight of her scoff at his inane question.

"I think it is because I was lying in your lap when I passed out—which was *after* you passed out." Apparently everything was a competition for her.

"Carmen." It had to be.

"Carmen? Is that the name of your lover?"

"No. It's the name of my fellow crew chief on the Night Stalkers' helo. It is exactly the sort of thing she would do to 'mess' with me: see us lying together and tell the med team we were a couple."

"It sounds like something a former lover would do to make you uncomfortable. Is she very sexy, this Carmen? All dark and Spanish?"

"Yes. No. She—" George let out an exasperated breath. "Carmen is redheaded, very American. Yes, very sexy. And no, she was never my lover."

"Is something wrong with you?"

"Yes, I'm missing part of my arm."

"I mean with you not taking this sexy redheaded Carmen as a lover."

"She is also married to the helo's copilot." Another strangeness to the Night Stalkers 5E. Their company was some sort of experiment where couples were allowed to fly together—which worked amazingly well in his estimation. It was so unusual, that he wasn't even sure if he should mention it to his commander when he returned to the 7th Squadron. Or if he'd be believed.

"Oh," was all the woman lying near him in the dark said. No surprise, merely acknowledgement. She was French, freer with the whole 'lover' concept, so perhaps that explained it.

He contemplated different British ways to present it. Maybe it was something that could only work in America.

Before he could ask for her thoughts, he heard the woman's breathing shift back into sleep. He wasn't far behind her.

6

"Two weeks' convalescence." Marta balanced on her crutches and blinked at the brilliant Aruban sunshine from beneath the shaded entrance of the hospital. The sun that had come in through their room's window had seemed so inviting. Out here, it was a blinding affront.

"Did you opt for home or the hotel?"

They had offered them the option. No more willing to explain herself to Mother than to anyone else, she'd opted to stay in Aruba. She held up the room key they'd issued her.

The Brit held up a room key as well. Thankfully with a different number.

But later that evening, as she sat alone and wondered what to do with herself—Aruba television broadcast mostly in Dutch—a knock sounded on her door.

"I'm not much of a cook one-handed," he had greeted her.

"I'm not much of a cook at all." Thankfully, he

made no wisecrack about French women who couldn't cook. She had heard it a thousand-and-one times, about a thousand beyond her tolerance level.

"I'll buy you dinner."

And just that simply, it had set the pattern. Physical therapy in the mornings, lunch by the hotel's pool, afternoons chatting quietly over bizarre tropical drinks in the shade of a thatched hut by the turquoise sea, and dinner in a different restaurant each night.

For three days they had declared that the six hundred years of Anglo-French wars had not ended with Napoleon's defeat in 1815. Though her companion had preferred to argue it began even two centuries earlier, as his people had fought in the Battle of Hastings in 1066, but that seemed a rather trite point to her.

To pass the time, they had decided to break any cross-channel armistice and resume hostile competition while here on the Aruban beaches—each fought hard to convince the other of the places they must visit. By the end of their "battle" she had a list of places in the British countryside that sounded lovely and he had a list of French restaurants to try from Chartres to Bordeaux.

Over the days, his interest in American idiom had turned to French idiom—which would have been easier to explain if he spoke any French. But he was a wise man. He had pursued it especially during physical therapy sessions which had been a very welcome distraction.

The first time they made love had almost been inevitable. She'd had a particularly tough physical therapy session that day and couldn't find the energy to leave the room. Being the noble, one-armed gentleman that he had proved himself to be, he had gone out to a local Bavarian restaurant and returned with beer-and-cheese soup, chicken schnitzel, and Black Forest cake. Maybe it was the tiered layers of rich, dark chocolate that had caused her to succumb. Perhaps it was how long she'd been without a man—she chose her lovers carefully and rarely.

He had risen to clear the table and she had pulled him back down for a chocolate-rich kiss. He might be one-handed and she one-legged, but the results were spectacular.

It became a regular part of their therapy. Practiced happily at rising in the morning, going to bed at night, and more rather than less often with a meal.

He was a gentle lover, something new in her experience. And very, very inventive.

"I thought you were British."

"That does not imply a lack of interest in sex. I simply don't brag about it to every person I meet. Though you offer a great deal to brag about, fair lady."

And there it was again. For reasons that eluded her, after waking up together in the same hospital room as a couple, they had never introduced themselves by name. At first it had felt awkward, *I almost died in your lap, but I don't know your name.*

Then during the "declared war" it had become a point of honor to ask nothing of their past, including their name. After the war, but before the sex, they had talked of past and family in ways she never had before. The sole offspring of an unwed mother who was also devoutly Catholic and had seen her daughter as both a sin and a blessing—and constant evidence of her own failings. He, the renegade son who had dropped out of

Oxford to enter the military rather than pursuing a posting to the foreign office.

Somehow, revealing so much of her past had been easier without having a name. She was able to speak of herself as if she was someone else. How she had spent her entire life trying to prove herself to others because she could never do so to her mother. Or herself. The impossibly deep answers drew them together in such unexpected ways until she felt closer to him than she had with any other—man or woman.

And now, having a nameless lover, had allowed them to discuss past lovers and past failures with equal anonymity. It also added a spice that neither of them appeared interested in losing.

## 7

The taxi to Queen Beatrix International Airport was desperately silent and George didn't know how to break it.

"We French are pragmatists."

The relief was so great that George almost cried out when she spoke. "I don't want to be pragmatic, practical, or any other p-word about you."

"We French have no choice but to be that way, with our country trapped between Germany, Italy, and Spain."

"Not to mention occasional British incursions." He couldn't help reminding her. They traded brief smiles about their "war" as the lovely Aruba seaside slid by wholly unattended.

"Some of those incursions were most enjoyable." And her smile was brighter at the memory of the lovemaking.

For that's what it had been. Sex between two injured soldiers had become lovemaking. Last night, knowing it was their last, every gesture had seemed so full of meaning that not a single word had been spoken. That had to be what making love felt like, for he'd never experienced anything else like it.

"There are vacations, the occasional leave…" the joy disappeared from her voice as she listed the options he too had thought of.

"We could both run off and join the French Foreign Legion."

It was understood that neither of them were willing to leave their service. Unable to say anything else, they simply clung to each other for the long thirteen-hour transit from Aruba to Heathrow via Miami. She had a medical upgrade to First Class for her leg, and he had simply paid for it out of pocket—half a month's pay, but worth every farthing.

She laid over with him for two days in London at his parents' townhouse.

Mother had fussed and Father had simply watched them as unreadably as ever.

8

---

*M*arta wasn't happy with feeling like a bug targeted by a rifle's laser-red sighting pointer. The townhouse was even more posh than their accents—a far cry from the flat above Mama's pastry shop. Marta also wasn't happy that she'd finally had to give up her first name to meet his parents.

They were Marta and George now. It took something away from them that she couldn't identify. She wanted it back, that cloak of anonymity that she had worn for two wonderful weeks. Names made something already terribly important, even more so.

With George's mother saying, "Marta this…" and "Marta that…" she felt cornered by the simple kindness of a fine hostess.

Alone together in George's room, neither of them used the other's name—not once—but it was only the slightest of respites. The end hung like doom itself on her plane ticket and the orders calling for her to report in.

It was their last day together. "Her Brit" had fallen

back asleep after their morning loving and she had crept out in search of coffee and a sweet roll. The house seemed echoingly silent so she tip-toed into the kitchen as quietly as she could with her cane, and spoiled all of her efforts with a yelp of surprise.

George Senior sat at the small walnut kitchen table in the steel-and-granite kitchen with a newspaper, but he was watching her. He had the same dark eyes as his son. And the same burning intelligence.

Marta offered a careful greeting smile, poured her coffee, but was unsure what to do next.

He nodded to the seat opposite him so, at a loss, she sat down as normally as she could manage—then dropped her cane so loudly on the floor that she almost jumped out of her skin.

"You are clearly in the same line of work as my son. Both wounded at the same time, on an international mission together that ended in Aruba."

She startled. How much did this stern, closed man know about his son's duties—which were supposed to be secret? Then she recalled that the tags on their luggage would have given that much away. So, she nodded and sipped her coffee.

"I have never seen him both so happy and so sad at the same time."

"It's like an ache in the chest that will never go away." That didn't sound like the Marta she knew, but it was true.

He folded his paper neatly and set it aside before looking her directly in the eye. It seemed that he was the darker version of his son. His coloring was much the same, but George's easy smile was lacking.

"I'm not very pleased with the concept of my son and daughter-in-law living in harm's way."

"Daughter-in law? We're not—" But his unflinching gaze said that he knew things she hadn't dared hope for. Or even think about. The image of the two of them together had so haunted her waking thoughts that it had moved into her dreams.

Married to George? She could think of no other she'd prefer…ever!

"We're soldiers, your son and I." It was something no civilian could truly understand. "We joined to serve. We both entered Special Forces because we wanted to make the greatest impact possible with our lives." It was one of the things she'd come to most respect in George. She had dismissed him for "being done" but had since learned there couldn't be a thought further from his mind. He had become as committed to the Night Stalkers as he had to his own unit and he felt the pain of loyalty.

"You were both on inter-force exchange programs." George's father didn't make it a question.

"Different ones that happened to coincide at the wrong moment. Or perhaps the best moment, because he saved my life."

George Senior gathered up his newspaper and his coffee cup and moved to the sink to rinse it out.

She glanced down and saw a blue file remained on the table. It had no markings but a code number on the tab. "Sir, you left behind a file."

He looked right at her across the length of the kitchen. "I don't know what you're talking about. I *always* know exactly where all of my classified documents are." Then he left the room.

She heard the front door open, then close as he greeted his driver.

Very slowly, she turned the file to face her. His intent was clear, but still her hands were shaking as she, feeling as if she was risking her life yet again, opened the file.

## 9

"It is you who saved my life," George whispered in her ear.

"How do you figure that?"

"Without you, my heart would never have known what it was missing."

"Perhaps it was your father, George Senior, who saved us both."

George still couldn't believe that. Somehow Marta had won Father over just as she had conquered himself. (France 2. Britain 0. He really must get back in the game.)

He held her hand tightly as they crossed the carpark and joined the loose queue of people heading into "The Doughnut." The circular Government Communications Headquarters was indeed shaped like the massive American doughnut lying on its side. He was going to work inside an American idiom.

The agency Father had never spoken of in all of his years was Five Eyes. It was an intelligence sharing organization that included: the Brits (the UK, along with Australia, New Zealand, and Canada) and the Yanks.

Another organization, Nine Eyes, ran by slightly different rules but with a similar purpose. It added on Denmark, Norway, the Netherlands, and—thank all the powers-that-be—France. The operation had been overjoyed at the addition of two fully cleared, field-trained operatives with experience embedding within their allies' forces.

"I have just one question," he leaned in to whisper in her ear.

"Yes?" Her voice was pure, lush tease.

"What is your last name? The wedding is this weekend and I think I should know my wife's last name before I marry her."

"You didn't read the invitations?"

"That rather seemed like cheating."

Marta stopped him by their joined hands, turned into his arms, and kissed him so thoroughly that reporting to their new job fell several places on his priority list. It also earned him a severe throat clearing from Father who he'd forgotten was walking in the crowd close behind them.

"Proulx," his father said, and moved on ahead of them. "It means Valiant."

"Valiant," George whispered. "Of course you saved my life."

"Sergeant George slayed the heart of the French dragoon," she murmured into his ear as he held her.

"And as a reward, he won the heart of the princess."

"He did."

She sighed happily in his arms one last time before

they turned hand-in-hand and—just like in her dream—walked forward together.

## LAST WORDS

Writing the 5E novels and stories was a grand adventure.

But it feels as if I've completed that journey.

It's a curious sensation as a writer to say goodbye to a series. Yet somehow, it's simply time.

I had considered continuing these tales, but that concept of the diamond-in-the-rough and the evolution of a person and a team led me in a whole new direction —my Miranda Chase action-adventure thrillers.

This happened in part before I noticed that the 5E stories, and especially the 5E novels, were at least as reliant on the action as the romance. I had started out with the romance being way at the front, but that had slowly shifted for me and I think that the Night Stalkers 5E were the pinnacle of that shift.

I was left with a choice, to either tip back into the more romantic side of my writing, or to follow that passion for action-adventure and see where it led me. I followed action-adventure.

Though I'm a long way from done with writing romance, I think the 5E's final mission delivered me to the perfect spot to start my next missions: *Drone, Thunderbolt, Condor, Ghostrider…*

Hope you enjoyed the flight!

# IF YOU LIKED THIS, YOU'LL LOVE:

*Four novels in one glorious set. Exclusively at:*
*www.buchmanbookworks.com*

# TARGET OF THE HEART (EXCERPT)

Major Pete Napier hovered his MH-47G Chinook helicopter ten kilometers outside of Lhasa, Tibet and a mere two inches off the tundra. A mixed action team of Delta Force and The Activity—the slipperiest intel group on the planet—flung themselves aboard.

The additional load sent an infinitesimal shift in the cyclic control in his right hand. The hydraulics to close the rear loading ramp hummed through the entire frame of the massive helicopter. By the time his crew chief could reach forward to slap an "all secure" signal against his shoulder, they were already ten feet up and fifty out. That was enough altitude. He kept the nose down as he clawed for speed in the thin air at eleven thousand feet.

"Totally worth it," one of the D-boys announced as soon as he was on the Chinook's internal intercom.

He'd have to remember to tell that to the two Black Hawks flying guard for him...when they were in a friendly country and could risk a radio transmission. This deep inside China—or rather Chinese-held territory as the CIA's mission-briefing spook had insisted on calling it—radios attracted attention and were only used to avoid imminent death and destruction.

"Great, now I just need to get us out of this alive."

"Do that, Pete. We'd appreciate it."

He wished to hell he had a stealth bird like the one that had gone into bin Laden's compound. But the one that had crashed during that raid had been blown up. Where there was one, there were always two, but the second had gone back into hiding as thoroughly as if it had never existed. He hadn't heard a word about it since.

The Tibetan terrain was amazing, even if all he could see of it was the monochromatic green of night vision. And blackness. The largest city in Tibet lay a mere ten kilometers away and they were flying over barren wilderness. He could crash out here and no one would know for decades unless some yak herder stumbled upon them. Or were yaks in Mongolia? He was a corn-fed, white boy from Colorado, what did he know about Tibet? Most of the countries he'd flown into on black ops missions he'd only seen at night anyway.

While moving very, very fast.

Like now.

The inside of his visor was painted with overlapping readouts. A pre-defined terrain map, the best that modern satellite imaging could build made the first layer. This wasn't some crappy, on-line, look-at-a-picture-of-your-house display. Someone had a pile of dung outside their goat pen? He could see it, tell you how high it was, and probably say if they were pygmy goats or full-size LaManchas by the size of their shit-pellets if he zoomed in.

On top of that were projected the forward-looking infrared camera images. The **FLIR** imaging gave him a real-time overlay, in case someone had put an addition onto their goat shed since the last satellite pass, or parked their tractor across his intended flight path.

His nervous system was paying autonomic attention to that combined landscape. He also compensated for the thin air at altitude as he instinctively chose when to start his climb over said goat shed or his swerve around it.

It was the third layer, the tactical display that had most of his attention. At least he and the two Black Hawks flying escort on him were finally on the move.

To insert this deep into Tibet, without passing over Bhutan or Nepal, they'd had to add wingtanks on the Black Hawks' hardpoints where he'd much rather have a couple banks of Hellfire missiles. Still, they had 20mm chain guns and the crew chiefs had miniguns which was some comfort.

While the action team was busy infiltrating the capital city and gathering intelligence on the particularly brutal Chinese assistant administrator, he and his crews had been squatting out in the wilderness under a camouflage net designed to make his helo look like just another god-forsaken Himalayan lump of granite.

Command had determined that it was better for the helos to wait on site through the day than risk flying out and back in. He and his crew had stood shifts on guard duty, but none of them had slept. They'd been flying together too long to have any new jokes, so they'd played a lot of cribbage. He'd long ago ruled no gambling on a mission, after a fistfight had broken out about a bluff hand that cost a Marine three hundred and forty-seven dollars. Marines hated losing to Army no matter how many times it happened. They'd had to sit on him for a long time before he calmed down.

Tonight's mission was part of an on-going campaign to discredit the Chinese "presence" in Tibet on the international stage—as if occupying the country the last sixty years didn't count toward ruling, whether invited or not. As usual, there was a crucial vote coming up at the U.N.—that, as usual, the Chinese could be guaranteed to ignore. However, the ever-hopeful CIA was in a hurry to make sure that any damaging information that they could validate was disseminated as thoroughly as possible prior to the vote.

Not his concern.

His concern was, were they going to pass over some Chinese sentry post at their top speed of a hundred and ninety-six miles an hour? The sentries would then call down a couple Shenyang J-16 jet fighters that could hustle along at Mach 2 to fry his sorry ass. He knew there was a pair of them parked at Lhasa along with some older gear that would be just as effective against his three helos.

"Don't suppose you could get a move on, Pete?"

"Eat shit, Nicolai!" He was a good man to have as a copilot. Pete knew he was holding on too tight, and Nicolai knew that a joke was the right way to ease the moment.

He, Nicolai, and the four pilots in the two Black

Hawks had a long way to go tonight and he'd never make it if he stayed so tight on the controls that he could barely maneuver. Pete eased off and felt his fingers tingle with the rush of returning blood. They dove down into gorges and followed them as long as they dared. They hugged cliff walls at every opportunity to decrease their radar profile. And they climbed.

That was the true danger—they would be up near the helos' limits when they crossed over the backbone of the Himalayas in their rush for India. The air was so rarefied that they burned fuel at a prodigious rate. Their reserve didn't allow for any extended battles while crossing the border…not for any battle at all really.

---

It was pitch dark outside her helicopter when Captain Danielle Delacroix stamped on the left rudder pedal while giving the big Chinook right-directed control on the cyclic. It tipped her most of the way onto her side, but let her continue in a straight line. A Chinook's rotors were sixty feet across—front to back they overlapped to make the spread a hundred feet long. By cross-controlling her bird to tip it, she managed to execute a straight line between two mock pylons only thirty feet apart. They were made of thin cloth so they wouldn't down the helo if you sliced one—she was the only trainee to not have cut one yet.

At her current angle of attack, she took up less than a half-rotor of width, just twenty-four feet. That left her nearly three feet to either side, sufficient as she was moving at under a hundred knots.

The training instructor sitting beside her in the copilot's seat didn't react as she swooped through the training course at Fort Campbell, Kentucky. Only child of a single mother, she was used to providing her own feedback loops, so she didn't expect anything else. Those who expected outside validation rarely survived the SOAR induction testing, never mind the two years of training that followed.

As a loner kid, Danielle had learned that self-motivated congratulations and fun were much easier to come by than external ones. She'd spent innumerable hours deep in her mind as a pre-teen superheroine. At twenty-nine she was well on her way to becoming a real life one, though Helo-girl had never been a character she'd thought of in her youth.

External validation or not, after two years of training with the U.S. Army's 160th Special Operations Aviation Regiment she was ready for some action. At least *she* was convinced that she was. But the trainers of Fort Campbell, Kentucky had not signed off on anyone in her trainee class yet. Nor had they given any hint of when they might.

She ducked ten tons of racing Chinook under a bridge and bounced into a near vertical climb to clear the power line on the far side. Like a ride on the toboggan at Terrassee Dufferin during *Le Carnaval de Québec,* only with five thousand horsepower at her fingertips. Using her Army signing bonus—the first money in her life that was truly hers—to attend *Le Carnaval* had been her one trip back after her birthplace since her mother took them to America when she was ten.

To even apply to SOAR required five years of prior military rotorcraft experience. She had applied after seven years because of a chance encounter—or rather what she'd thought was a chance encounter at the time.

Captain Justin Roberts had been a top Chinook pilot, the one who had convinced her to switch from her beloved Black Hawk and try out the massive twin-rotor craft. One flight and she'd been a goner, begging her commander until he gave in and let her cross over to the new platform. Justin had made the jump from the 10th Mountain Division to the 160th SOAR not long after that.

Then one night she'd been having pizza in Watertown, New York a couple miles off the 10th's base at Fort Drum.

"Danielle?" Justin had greeted her with the surprise of finding a good friend in an unexpected place. Danielle had liked Justin—even if he was a too-tall, too-handsome cowboy and completely knew it. But "good friend" was unusual for Danielle, with anyone, and Justin came close.

"Captain Roberts," as a dry greeting over the top edge of her Suzanne Brockmann novel didn't faze him in the slightest.

"Mind if I join ya?" A question he then answered for himself by sliding into the opposite seat and taking a slice of her pizza. She been thinking of taking the leftovers back to base, but that was now an idle thought.

"Are you enjoying life in SOAR?" she did her best to appear a normal, social human, a skill she'd learned by rote. *Greeting someone you knew after a time apart? Ask a question about them.* "They treating you well?"

"Whoo-ee, you have no idea, Danielle," his voice was smooth as…well, always…so she wouldn't think about it also sounding like a pickup line. He was beautiful, but didn't interest her; the outgoing ones never did.

"Tell me." *Men love to talk about themselves, so let them.*

And he did. But she'd soon forgotten about her novel, and would have forgotten the pizza if he hadn't reminded her to eat.

His stories shifted from intriguing to fascinating. There was a world out there that she'd been only peripherally aware of. The Night Stalkers of the 160th SOAR weren't simply better helicopter pilots, they were the most highly-trained and best-equipped ones on the planet. Their missions were pure razor's edge and black-op dark.

He'd left her with a hundred questions and enough interest to fill out an application to the 160th. Being a decent guy, Justin even paid for the pizza after eating half.

The speed at which she was rushed into testing told her that her meeting with Justin hadn't been by chance and that she owed him more than half a pizza next time they met. She'd asked after him a couple of times since she'd made it past the qualification exams—and the examiners' brutal interviews that had left her questioning her sanity, never mind her ability.

"Justin Roberts is presently deployed, ma'am," was the only response she'd ever gotten.

Now that she was through training—almost, had to be soon, didn't it?—Danielle realized that was probably less of an evasion and more likely to do with the brutal op tempo the Night Stalkers maintained. The SOAR 1st Battalion had just won the coveted Lt. General Ellis D. Parker awards for Outstanding Combat Aviation Battalion *and* Aviation Battalion of the Year. They'd been on deployment every single day of the last year, actually of the last decade-plus since 9/11.

The very first Special Forces boots on the ground in Afghanistan were delivered that October by the Night Stalkers and nothing had slacked off since. Justin might be in the 5th battalion D company, but they were just as heavily assigned as the 1st.

Part of their training had included tours in Afghanistan. But unlike their prior deployments, these were brief, intense, and then they'd be back in the States pushing to integrate their new skills.

SOAR needed her training to end and so did she.

Danielle was ready for the job, in her own, inestimable opinion. But she wasn't going to get there until the trainers signed off that she'd reached fully mission-qualified proficiency.

The Fort Campbell training course was never set up the same from one flight to the next, but it always had a time limit. The time would be short and they didn't tell you what it was. So she drove the Chinook for all it was worth like Regina Jaquess waterskiing her way to U.S. Ski Team Female Athlete of the Year.

The Night Stalkers were a damned secretive lot, and after two years of training, she understood why. With seven years flying for the 10th, she'd thought she was good.

She'd been repeatedly lauded as one of the top pilots at Fort Drum.

The Night Stalkers had offered an education in what it really meant to fly. In the two years of training, she'd flown more hours than in the seven years prior, despite two deployments to Iraq. And spent more time in the classroom than her life-to-date accumulated flight hours.

But she was ready now. It was *très viscérale,* right down in her bones she could feel it. The Chinook was as much a part of her nervous system as breathing.

Too bad they didn't build men they way they built the big Chinooks—especially the MH-47G which were built specifically to SOAR's requirements. The aircraft were steady, trustworthy, and the most immensely powerful helicopters deployed in the U.S. Army—what more could a girl ask for? But finding a superhero man to go with her superhero helicopter was just a fantasy for a lonely teenage girl.

She dove down into a canyon and slid to a hover mere inches over the reservoir inside the thirty-second window laid out on the flight plan.

Danielle resisted a sigh. She was ready for something to happen and to happen soon.

---

PETE'S CHINOOK and his two escort Black Hawks crossed into the mountainous province of Sikkim, India ten feet over the glaciers and still moving fast. It was an hour before dawn, they'd made it out of China while it was still dark.

"Twenty minutes of fuel remaining," Nicolai said it like a personal challenge when they hit the border.

"Thanks, I never would have noticed."

It had been a nail-biting tradeoff: the more fuel he burned, the more easily he climbed due to the lighter load. The more he climbed, the faster he burned what little fuel remained.

Safe in Indian airspace he climbed hard as Nicolai counted down the minutes remaining, burning fuel even faster than he had been while crossing the mountains of southern Tibet. They caught up with the U.S. Air Force HC-130P Combat King refueling tanker with only ten minutes of fuel left.

"Ram that bitch," Nicolai called out.

Pete extended the refueling probe which reached only a few feet beyond the forward edge of the rotor blade and drove at the basket trailing behind the tanker on its long hose.

He nailed it on the first try despite the fluky winds. Striking the valve in the basket with over four hundred pounds of pressure, a clamp snapped over the refueling probe and Jet A fuel shot into his tanks.

His helo had the least fuel due to having the most men aboard, so he was first in line. His Number Two picked up the second refueling basket trailing off the other wing of the Combat King. Thirty seconds and three hundred gallons later and he was breathing much more easily.

"Ah," Nicolai sighed. "It is better than the sex," his thick Russian accent only ever surfaced in this moment or in a bar while picking up women.

"Hey, Nicolai," Nicky the Greek called over the intercom from his crew chief position seated behind Pete. "Do you make love in Russian?"

A question Pete had always been careful to avoid.

"For you, I make special exception." That got a laugh over the system.

Which explained why Pete always kept his mouth shut at this moment.

"The ladies, Nicolai? What about the ladies?" Alfie the portside gunner asked.

"Ah," he sighed happily as he signaled that the other choppers had finished their refueling and formed up to either side, "the ladies love the Russian. They don't need to know I grew up in Maryland and I learn my great-great-grandfather's native tongue at the University called Virginia."

He sounded so pleased that Pete wished he'd done the same rather than study Japanese and Mandarin.

Another two hours of—thank god—straight-and-level flight at altitude through the breaking dawn and they landed on the aircraft carrier awaiting them in the Bay of Bengal. India had agreed to turn a blind eye as long as the Americans never actually touched their soil.

Once standing on the deck—and the worst of the kinks worked out—he pulled his team together: six pilots and seven crew chiefs.

"Honor to serve!" He saluted them sharply.

"Hell yeah!" They shouted in response and saluted in turn. It was their version of spiking the football in the end zone.

A petty officer in a bright green vest appeared at his elbow, "Follow me please, sir." He pointed toward the Navy-gray command structure that towered above the carrier's deck. The Commodore of the entire carrier group was waiting for him just outside the entrance. Not a good idea to keep a One-Star waiting, so he waved at the team.

"See you in the mess for dinner," he shouted to the crew over the noise of an F-18 Hornet fighter jet trapping on the #2 wire. After two days of surviving on MREs while squatting on the Tibetan tundra, he was ready for a steak, a burger, a mountain of pasta, whatever. Or maybe all three.

The green escorted him across the hazards of the busy flight deck. Pete had kept his helmet on to buffer the noise, but even at that he winced as another Hornet fired up and was flung aloft by the catapult.

"Orders, Major Napier," the Commodore handed him a folded sheet the moment he arrived. "Hate to lose you."

The Commodore saluted, which Pete automatically returned before looking down at the sheet of paper in his hands. The man was gone before the import of Pete's orders slammed in.

A different green-clad deckhand showed up with Pete's duffle bag and began guiding him toward a loading C-2 Greyhound twin-prop airplane. It was parked number two for the launch catapult, close behind the raised jet-blast deflector.

His crew, being led across in the opposite direction to return to the berthing decks below, looked at him aghast.

"Stateside," was all he managed to gasp out as they passed.

A stream of foul cursing followed him from behind. Their crew was tight. Why the hell was Command breaking it up?

And what in the name of fuck-all had he done to deserve this?

He glanced at the orders again as he stumbled up the Greyhound's rear ramp and crash landed into a seat.

Training rookies?

It was worse than a demotion.

This was punishment.

---

*Get all 4 novels now in a complete set exclusively at:*
*www.buchmanbookworks.com*

# ABOUT THE AUTHOR

USA Today and Amazon #1 Bestseller M. L. "Matt" Buchman has 60+ action-adventure thrillers, and contemporary and military romance novels. Also 100 short stories and lotsa audiobooks.

Booklist says: 3X "Top 10 Romance of the Year" and among "The 20 Best Romantic Suspense Novels: Modern Masterpieces." NPR and B&N say "Best 5 Romance of the Year." *Publishers Weekly* wrote: "Tom Clancy fans open to a strong female lead will clamor for more."

A project manager with a geophysics degree, he's designed and built houses, flown and jumped out of planes, solo-sailed a 50' sailboat, and bicycled solo around the world…and he quilts. More at: www.mlbuchman.com.

**Other works by M. L. Buchman:** (* - also in audio)

## Thrillers

### Dead Chef
*One Chef!*
*Two Chef!*

### Miranda Chase
*Drone**
*Thunderbolt**
*Condor**
*Ghostrider**

## Romantic Suspense

### Delta Force
*Target Engaged**
*Heart Strike**
*Wild Justice**
*Midnight Trust**

### Firehawks
**MAIN FLIGHT**
*Pure Heat*
*Full Blaze*
*Hot Point**
*Flash of Fire**
*Wild Fire*
**SMOKEJUMPERS**
*Wildfire at Dawn**
*Wildfire at Larch Creek**
*Wildfire on the Skagit**

### The Night Stalkers
**MAIN FLIGHT**
*The Night Is Mine*
*I Own the Dawn*
*Wait Until Dark*
*Take Over at Midnight*
*Light Up the Night*
*Bring On the Dusk*
*By Break of Day*

**AND THE NAVY**
*Christmas at Steel Beach*
*Christmas at Peleliu Cove*
**WHITE HOUSE HOLIDAY**
*Daniel's Christmas**
*Frank's Independence Day**
*Peter's Christmas**
*Zachary's Christmas**
*Roy's Independence Day**
*Damien's Christmas**
**5E**
*Target of the Heart*
*Target Lock on Love*
*Target of Mine*
*Target of One's Own*

### Shadow Force: Psi
*At the Slightest Sound**
*At the Quietest Word**

### White House Protection Force
*Off the Leash**
*On Your Mark**
*In the Weeds**

## Contemporary Romance

### Eagle Cove
*Return to Eagle Cove*
*Recipe for Eagle Cove*
*Longing for Eagle Cove*
*Keepsake for Eagle Cove*

### Henderson's Ranch
*Nathan's Big Sky**
*Big Sky, Loyal Heart**
*Big Sky Dog Whisperer**

### Love Abroad
*Heart of the Cotswolds: England*
*Path of Love: Cinque Terre, Italy*

# Other works by M. L. Buchman:

### Contemporary Romance (cont)

**Where Dreams**
*Where Dreams are Born*
*Where Dreams Reside*
*Where Dreams Are of Christmas*
*Where Dreams Unfold*
*Where Dreams Are Written*

### Science Fiction / Fantasy

**Deities Anonymous**
*Cookbook from Hell: Reheated*
*Saviors 101*

**Single Titles**
*The Nara Reaction*
*Monk's Maze*
*the Me and Elsie Chronicles*

### Non-Fiction

**Strategies for Success**
*Managing Your Inner Artist/Writer*
*Estate Planning for Authors*
*Character Voice*


# Short Story Series by M. L. Buchman:

### Romantic Suspense

**Delta Force**
*Delta Force*

**Firehawks**
*The Firehawks Lookouts*
*The Firehawks Hotshots*
*The Firebirds*

**The Night Stalkers**
*The Night Stalkers*
*The Night Stalkers 5E*
*The Night Stalkers CSAR*
*The Night Stalkers Wedding Stories*

**US Coast Guard**
*US Coast Guard*

**White House Protection Force**
*White House Protection Force*

### Contemporary Romance

**Eagle Cove**
*Eagle Cove*

**Henderson's Ranch**
*Henderson's Ranch*

**Where Dreams**
*Where Dreams*

### Thrillers

**Dead Chef**
*Dead Chef*

### Science Fiction / Fantasy

**Deities Anonymous**
*Deities Anonymous*

**Other**
*The Future Night Stalkers*
*Single Titles*